KING CITY

Author photograph by Linda Woods

Printed in the United States of America.

Published by Thomas & Mercer
P.O. Box 400818
Las Vegas, NV 89140

ISBN-13: 9781612183176
ISBN-10: 1612183174

KING CITY

by LEE GOLDBERG

THOMAS & MERCER

CHAPTER ONE

Tom Wade was asleep in bed beside his wife when the call came. He had a pretty good idea what the call was about before he answered the phone. He'd been dreading it for the last few days.

"Yeah," he whispered, rolling over onto his back.

Alison stirred and grumbled something unintelligible.

"We moved on all of them thirty minutes ago." It was Carl Pinkus, the prosecutor Wade had been working with at the Justice Department.

Wade checked the alarm clock. It was 2:00 a.m. The green glow of the numbers glinted off his badge on the nightstand.

He could guess how it went down. All across the city, strike teams made up of FBI and ATF agents kicked down the doors at the homes of all seven men at precisely the same instant, hoping to surprise them in bed, naked and defenseless.

It was standard operating procedure in situations like this, designed to minimize risk and prevent any of the targets from being warned that the law was coming for them.

It usually worked.

"You could have waited until morning to tell me," Wade said, sitting up.

"It is morning," Pinkus said.

"What went wrong?" Wade asked. His wife was wide-awake now—he could tell from her breathing.

"I'm outside of Roger Malden's place. He wants to see you, Tom."

"I've got nothing to say to him."

"He must have something real important to say to you," Pinkus said. "He's holding his wife and kids hostage, and if you don't get your ass down here now, he's going to kill them."

"I'll be there in four minutes," Wade said and hung up the phone.

Roger lived two miles away in a tract home with the same floor plan as Wade's. They even had the same pool man. That wasn't all that they had in common.

He threw back the sheets, stood up naked, and went to the easy chair where he'd draped the clothes he'd been wearing last night—a sweatshirt and a pair of jeans. He could feel Alison's eyes on his back. He pulled his sweatshirt over his head.

Wade was six feet tall, fit and lean. He had the hands of a man who worked with them—wielding an ax, a shovel, or a pick—but that came more from heredity than it did from hard labor, though he'd done his share of that before he became a cop.

"What is it?" she asked.

Alison was used to the late-night calls but not the troubled undercurrent that was in Wade's voice during the short conversation. He knew that she'd pick up on it.

"A hostage situation," he said, turning to look at her as he pulled up his pants and buckled his belt.

Alison was sitting up, not bothering to cover her nakedness. Wade couldn't have a discussion naked and uncovered, but she was totally comfortable with it. In the semidarkness, she looked just the way she did the first night that they'd slept together twenty years ago.

"You're not a hostage negotiator," she said.

He hadn't planned to tell her about it like this. For weeks, he'd been rehearsing exactly what he was going to say, how he would explain the two long years of subterfuge.

"It's Roger. He's threatening to kill his family."

Her breath caught in her throat. She shook her head. "No, I don't believe that. Not Roger."

"The FBI raided his house tonight, Ally. He's been indicted on corruption charges."

"That's crazy," she said. "He's a good man."

"They've arrested the entire Major Crimes Unit."

She stared at him, realization slowly dawning on her. "But they didn't come for you."

He reached for his badge. "We'll talk about this when I get back."

Wade hung the badge on a lanyard around his neck and hurried out. It felt like he was running away from her. He'd never run away from anything before.

———

Detective Roger Malden's two-story tract home was illuminated like a movie set, bathed in the harsh white glow from portable arc lights that had been brought in on trailers.

The residents of the adjoining homes had been cleared out and were being kept behind a police line at the end of the block.

Wade drove up in his department-issued Crown Vic, which might as well have been a badge on four wheels. The uniformed officers waved him through without a glance or a check of his ID. They looked confused. He couldn't blame them. They had no idea what was going on. Nobody in the department did.

He parked behind an FBI armored assault unit. As he got out of his car, he noted the sharpshooters on the rooftops and the Kevlar-vested agents crouched behind their vehicles, aiming their guns at Malden's house as if it might leap from its foundation and attack them.

Carl Pinkus was easy to spot among the agents. He wore a Kevlar vest over his suit and a tactical helmet on his head and was wielding his BlackBerry instead of a gun, firing off text messages with his thumbs. He pocketed the device when he saw Wade approach.

"What's the situation?" Wade asked.

"You're standing out in the open, asking to be shot," Pinkus said from behind a car. "Take cover."

"If I wanted cover, I would have stayed in bed."

"You didn't tell us that Roger is an insomniac."

"I didn't know."

"He saw the agents coming," Pinkus said. "He fired off some warning shots before we even got close. We think he's herded the family into the kitchen."

Wade nodded and started toward the house.

Pinkus grabbed him. "Put on a vest before you walk in there."

"You think that would make my head off-limits for him to shoot?"

"We need you alive to testify."

"Thanks for giving me something to live for."

Wade sauntered across the street and up the front walk as if he were going to another one of Roger's weekend barbecues. He knocked on the door.

"It's me," he yelled.

"Are you alone, Tom?" Roger asked in a loud voice from deep inside the house. Wade didn't hear panic or desperation underscoring his words. He heard bitterness.

"Yeah, but I'm carrying a gun in each hand and a stick of dynamite in my teeth."

"So am I. Come on in and we'll party."

Wade opened the door and stepped into the darkened house. Same floor plan but different furniture, electronics, and art.

Roger's stuff was more upscale and contemporary than what Wade had. But Wade didn't have Roger's money.

He walked to the kitchen. After every Walden barbecue, Ally always raved about their travertine floors, granite countertops, and stainless steel appliances.

Roger sat on the edge of the center island, near the stove top. He was wearing a terry cloth bathrobe over a T-shirt and drawstring pajama pants. He didn't have a stick of dynamite, but he was holding a Glock in each hand.

"I figured the traitor had to be you," Roger said. "You are always so fucking self-righteous, whether you're making an arrest or a sandwich."

Wade glanced to his right and saw Sally Malden and her daughters, ages nine and eleven, all in their nightgowns and huddling together on the floor, their legs curled up against their bodies. She held her daughters close to her, one under each arm. They were all crying silently, trails of tears and snot running down their faces.

He focused his gaze back on Roger. "You don't want to hurt your family. You want to hurt me. I'm here now. Let them go."

"They need to see this," he said.

"Please," Sally cried. "Think of the children."

"I am," he snapped, waving a gun in her direction. She tensed up, pulling the kids tighter to her bosom. "Why do you think I did it? So you could have the house you wanted, the clothes you wanted, *everything* you wanted."

"I didn't want this," she said.

"Only because you haven't seen it on HGTV. The damn channel was on twenty-four/seven in this house, just so you could constantly point out to me all the things we needed. You even had it on while we fucked."

"Only so the kids wouldn't hear us," she said.

"I couldn't take a shit without finding the latest issue of *Architectural Digest* waiting for me with the corners marked down on the pages you wanted me to see."

"This isn't my fault," she said.

"You didn't shake down the drug dealers or take any bribes, but you were part of it, honey. Don't kid yourself." He looked at Wade. "You took the money too, but I never saw you spend it on anything. You never enjoyed it. I asked myself about that and never came up with an answer."

"I gave it to the Justice Department."

"You didn't keep even a little of it for expenses?"

Wade shook his head.

"C'mon. Don't you have a mortgage? Don't you have things you need and want but can't afford?"

"Sure I do."

"You could have had them," Roger said. "You could have had prosperity."

"I could also be sitting in my kitchen waving a gun at my family and ranting about what I read in the bathroom."

"You're an asshole."

"So shoot me, Roger. It would be less painful than listening to any more of your whining."

"You suck as a hostage negotiator."

Wade shrugged. "I don't negotiate."

"Why did you sell us out? What did they offer you?"

"Nothing."

"Bullshit. Nobody does anything for nothing."

"It's my job to catch bad guys. You're a bad guy. It's as simple as that."

Roger nodded. "So you did it just so you could feel even more self-righteous than you already do."

"I did because that's what I am paid to do. It's what you're paid to do too. I guess you forgot about that. But it's not your fault, Roger. It's those bastards at *Architectural Digest*."

"You don't know what you've done, what it's going to mean for me, what it's going to mean to them," Roger tipped his head toward his family. "Did you ever think about the consequences, Tom? Even once?"

"Did you?"

Roger glared at Wade for a long moment, then aimed the gun in his right hand at his family. They whimpered in terror. He tossed the gun in his left hand to Wade, who caught it.

Wade checked to see if his gun was loaded. It was. "What's the game?"

"I'm going to blow my wife's head off in five seconds unless you shoot me."

"Suicide by cop," Wade said.

"I'm not going to let you hide behind a bunch of federal agents. If you want to take me down, you're going to have to do it yourself, right in front of my family so they can see the—"

Wade shot him in the right shoulder, knocking him off the counter onto the floor. The children screamed. He kicked away Roger's dropped gun, rolled him facedown on the blood-spattered travertine, and pinned his left arm behind his back.

"You're under arrest," Wade said.

Roger started to heave before Wade could read him his rights. Wade tipped him to one side so he wouldn't choke on his own vomit.

That's when FBI agents burst into the kitchen from every doorway. Two of the agents immediately hustled Sally Malden and her wailing kids away. But they still saw what a puking, mewling, bloody mess their father was and that Wade was holding him down.

11

It was their father who'd threatened to kill them, but it was Wade whom they hated. He saw it in their teary eyes already. The hate would only intensify with time.

Wade got up off Roger, handed his gun to one of the agents, and walked outside, the harsh glare of the arc lights casting his long shadow over the house.

CHAPTER TWO

King City was created by greed, and as far as Wade was concerned, it had permeated the place and its inhabitants ever since.

The city was conceived in the mid-1800s by four wealthy railroad, logging, and shipping barons as a means of expanding their already immense fortunes into the Pacific Northwest. They wanted a spot on a river that could be reached easily by a railroad extension and that was near land rich in agricultural, logging, and mineral possibilities.

They found what they were looking for in the heavily forested, rocky peaks of the West Hills and the verdant Chewelah River Valley in eastern Washington State.

The only problem was that the land was already inhabited by Native Americans. It had been their ancestral home for centuries before the white man ever showed up.

The obvious solution was war. But the businessmen knew from experience that it could be a time-consuming, messy, and expensive endeavor. So they relied on what they knew best.

Greed.

They offered the Indians barrels of whiskey and wagonloads of blankets and asked for nothing in return but friendship.

The Indians proudly draped themselves in their disease-infected blankets, guzzled down their poisonous raw alcohol, and basked in their riches.

The tribe was decimated by plague and liver disease within a matter of months, clearing the way for progress.

The four founding businessmen called their new metropolis King City in their own honor and named the major thoroughfares and parks for themselves individually. The other streets were named after presidents, generals, and other great leaders like themselves.

Wade walked east on Chandler Boulevard, the preferred address of the city's lawyers, to Riverfront Park, a grassy strip of bike paths and jogging trails that lined the shore from the Grant Street Bridge south to the Performing Arts Center.

It was a bright, sunny day that looked warmer than it actually was, the clear blue skies masking an unexpected chill. Nobody seemed to be dressed warmly enough for it, and that included Wade, in a short-sleeve polo shirt and jeans. It was a deceitful day.

There were picnic tables and benches facing the river. It was a popular place for picnics and parties on the weekends and, on weekdays, for the city workers in One King Plaza to gather for a smoke.

Chief Gavin Reardon was one of them. He wore a tailored suit and sat on top of a picnic table, his feet on the bench, smoking a cigarette and looking at the Grant Street Bridge, which resembled an enormous number eight made out of steel and lying sideways over the water.

The chief was a lifelong cop from a family of lifelong cops and ran the department as if it were his birthright. Perhaps it was. He was a star quarterback in college and could have gone pro, but he preferred a badge. At fifty-five years old, his hair was totally gray, and he still looked like he could run over a linebacker and keep right on going.

He hadn't spoken to Wade since that night at Roger's house. He'd immediately put Wade on indefinite paid administrative leave and told him not to get within a hundred yards of a King City police station.

Wade stayed on leave throughout the countless hours of depositions and testimony that stretched over the next two years as the Justice Department prepared and prosecuted its case, winning convictions against all seven of the cops. That last conviction came down only two days before this moment in the park.

The chief flicked his cigarette into the river as Wade approached.

"There was a time in this city when the police would hang the worst criminal offenders from the bridge and leave their corpses to rot as a warning to anyone who thought about disrespecting the law." The chief spoke without acknowledging Wade's presence with even a glance. "It was a very effective deterrent. Sometimes I miss those days."

Wade looked out at the bridge and imagined the corpses swinging on ropes over the river. Welcome to King City.

He shifted his gaze back to the chief. "They had a broad interpretation of disrespect," Wade said. "Men were hung for demanding safer working conditions in the factories."

"It kept the peace," the chief said.

"It was intimidation to prevent anyone from challenging the rampant corruption and abuse of authority."

"Those were violent, chaotic times. The law had to take a hard line to maintain order," the chief said. "As a result, King City was probably the safest, cleanest, and most productive city in America."

Wade sighed and put his hands in his pockets. "Is there a reason we aren't having this thrilling historical debate in your office?"

The chief turned to him, gave him the once-over, and frowned with disgust at what he saw.

"I wanted a smoke and it's against the law in public buildings. You might call the feds on me. Besides, the place is full of men with loaded weapons who'd like to shoot you. I'm pretty tempted right now myself."

"Gee, was it something I said?" Wade asked.

"I promoted you to the MCU because I thought you were made out of the right stuff. I didn't think you'd go crying like a little girl to the Justice Department the minute you saw some mischief."

"We aren't talking about hardworking cops stepping on a few civil rights or bending a few regulations to get the job done," Wade said. "They were taking bribes, extorting drug dealers for a cut of their action, skimming from the cash and drugs that they seized as evidence, and running a protection racket right out of police headquarters."

"You should have come to me," the chief said. "I would have handled it."

"You would have buried it."

"I would have done what was best for the department," the chief said. "That's our sworn duty."

"Our duty is to enforce the law."

"We *are* the law," the chief said.

Wade nodded. "That's why I went to the Justice Department."

"You spied for them for sixteen months, bugging conversations, taking pictures, stealing papers. You lied to everyone. Your fellow officers. Your family. And then you shot one of your own in his kitchen, right in front of his wife and kids."

"He was holding them hostage," Wade said.

"You drove him to it," the chief said. "All of that ugliness, all of the embarrassment you caused the department, would have been avoided if you'd just come to me. Instead, you betrayed us all. Even your wife can't stand to look at you anymore."

Wade took a deep breath and let it out slowly, trying to keep his rising anger in check. He wasn't going to let himself be baited.

"Seven detectives that you considered the best of the best are sitting in prison for the next twenty years," Wade said. "Apparently, you're a lousy judge of character, so you'll have to forgive me if I'm not all broken up about losing your respect. Are we done here?"

The chief's face reddened with rage. Wade looked him right in the eye, unapologetic and unbowed.

"Not yet," the chief said. "I'm launching a new community policing initiative by establishing substations staffed by a few uniformed officers in some of the city's most troubled areas. You're going to work in one of them."

"You're demoting me," Wade said.

"Hell no, I wouldn't do that," the chief said. "You might see that as retribution and use it as grounds for a lawsuit."

"So what's this?"

"A reassignment, a lateral move. You'll have the same rank, pay, and benefits as you do now." The chief picked up two files that were on the picnic table beside him and slid them toward Wade. "You'll have two officers under your command and we'll leave you alone."

That meant no support, no backup, stuck on his own in some urban Siberia.

"Where is this substation?"

The chief smiled. "Darwin Gardens."

Wade knew the place. Every cop did.

It was four miles from where Wade was standing, fifty miles from the lake where he grew up, and light-years away from anywhere any sane person would want to be.

It was the old industrial core of King City, bordered on the east by the rotting factories and docks along the river, by a Berlin wall of squalid apartment blocks to the south, and by the decaying railroad yards and the freeway to the west.

Darwin Gardens had the highest homicide rate in the city, but that was a dirty little secret that the chief, the police commission, and the chamber of commerce kept to themselves and didn't factor into the official stats.

The neighborhood was run by criminal warlords who operated with virtual impunity. Any cops who entered became chum for shooters looking for target practice. For the people who lived there, it was survival of the fittest—which was how the neighborhood had earned its nickname.

The city fathers ignored the problems there because it would cost far too much in blood and money to make a difference in a place that didn't matter. And because the people who voted, and paid the most taxes, and financed campaigns didn't live there anymore.

They'd start caring about Darwin Gardens only when the crime came to their doorsteps in Abbott Park, Meston Heights, or the swanky shops along McEveety Way.

Wade looked at the chief's big fat grin. "When did you start giving a damn about Darwin Gardens?"

"Not until I needed a shithole to put you in," the chief said.

CHAPTER THREE

The last time Wade wore his uniform was a few years earlier at a police funeral. Two rookie cops had chased a stolen car into a cul-de-sac in Darwin Gardens and an ambush. More than two hundred bullets were recovered from their vehicle and their obliterated bodies.

The police staged a massive crackdown, arrested anyone who didn't look middle class and white, and that was it. Things went back to the way they were before.

Wade wasn't going to a funeral today, although as far as Chief Reardon and the department were concerned, he was. His law enforcement career was dead and they wanted him to mourn his lost future every time he put on his uniform.

But Wade didn't look at things that way, not even now as he dressed in a dreary, fifty-bucks-a-night hotel room, most of his belongings in a padlocked storage unit across the street.

Wearing his blues, seeing that badge on his chest again, reinforced something essential about himself, but if you asked him what it was, he probably couldn't have found the words. Eloquence wasn't one of his qualities. He knew only that it felt right in a way few things in his life ever did.

If the chief thought that Wade would see this as an indignity, that it would make him quit and go away, it only showed how little he knew him, as if that hadn't been proved dramatically already.

He was proud of the uniform. It was why he did what he did and lost what he lost. His father taught him that standing up for what you believe in comes with a price but that backing down exacts a toll that your soul never stops paying.

It was customary, but not required, for King City police officers to wear a Kevlar vest under their uniforms. Most of them did. All Wade wore was the white T-shirt that he'd carefully ironed and lightly starched the night before.

He buckled on his duty belt and then looped the leather snaps known as "keepers" to the black belt that held up his pants. Four keepers were standard, two in the front of the duty belt and two in the back. But he'd had two extra ones added on either side of his holster to secure it more rigidly, making it easier for him to quickly and smoothly draw his Glock. He had another gun in an ankle holster, but he'd never had to use that one.

His duty belt also carried handcuffs, a cell phone, a collapsible baton, a tiny flashlight, and a canister of pepper spray, a piece of masking tape affixed to it that read, "Bat Shark Repellant," in Alison's handwriting, encircled by a rough approximation of the 1960s Batman logo. She'd put the tape on the canister in a playful moment years ago and he had no intention of peeling it off now.

A fully loaded duty belt weighed about twenty-five pounds. There were more cops on disability from the back strain of lugging around their equipment on their waists than from injuries sustained in assaults, shootings, or car accidents.

But Wade liked the extra weight.

It wasn't punishment for him to be putting on his blues again. It was more like therapy. It was exactly what he needed, now more than ever.

Wade was thirty-eight years old, but he felt and looked older. He was already seeing some strands of gray in his hair, though they were barely noticeable now that he'd trimmed it down to an almost military buzz cut.

Still, there was a depth in his gaze and a weathered sturdiness to his stature and gait that suggested he'd lived more years than he had, time that cut scars and built calluses with its hard passing, but that somehow were less evident when his badge was in his pocket and his daily uniform was an off-the-rack suit.

He took one last glance around the room to make sure everything was in order.

Before he'd dressed, he'd straightened up the bathroom, folded his towels, and made his bed, even though it was the cleaning lady's job. He hated to leave behind a mess.

Satisfied with what he saw, he picked up his briefcase, left the room, and took the stairs one flight down to the clean, contemporary, and totally charmless lobby.

It was decorated in a style that Alison would have called "Contemporary Motor Home." There were a couple of couches upholstered in cloth with the same floral pattern as the bedspread in his room, a TV set tuned to CNN, and some fake potted plants that looked more lifelike than the perpetually smiling young woman behind the Formica-paneled front counter.

The lobby opened up onto a small dining room, where guests were offered a free continental breakfast. Wade didn't know what was "continental" about dry toast, dry bagels, tiny boxes of dry cereal, and cubed pieces of canned fruit floating in an enormous salad bowl of sugary goop.

The breakfast offerings were awful, but the dining room was crowded every morning anyway with traveling businessmen and vacationing families.

Wade didn't understand why people would enthusiastically line up to eat something disgusting and inedible simply because it was free.

Dog crap was free too, but he wasn't going to eat it.

So he strode outside and across the parking lot toward the Denny's next door.

The sky was cloudless, but the blue was obscured by the toxic brown layer of carcinogens and greenhouse gases that hung over King City and seemed to get darker as it baked under the heat lamp of the unseasonably hot September sun. The weather was schizophrenic that month.

The hotel was tucked up against the weedy freeway embankment. At night in his room, Wade could hear the traffic rushing by outside his window. He didn't mind the noise. There was a pleasant rhythm to it, as natural in its own way as waves lapping at the shore.

The rhythm of the freeway traffic was faster in the morning, infused with the energy of a waking city. Beneath the beat, like a jazz riff, was the irregular, sometimes discordant whoosh of cars speeding by on the street. It was a beautiful noise, as Neil Diamond would say, not that Wade would ever admit to owning one of his albums, though he had them all. He could blame his father for that embarrassing flaw in his character.

Neil Diamond, Frank Sinatra, Tony Bennett, Tom Jones, Sammy Davis Jr., and Shirley Bassey were the only singers his father ever listened to.

He hated the music when he was a kid but found himself liking it as a man. Either he'd matured into it, the way the elderly age into using walkers, or he drew some kind of comfort from the nostalgia and the connection to his dad, which was the explanation he chose to accept.

The hotel and the Denny's were located in a light-industrial pocket of warehouses on the city's east side, midway between downtown and the suburbs of Clayton, Denton, and Tennyson, which were built on farmland that had been subdivided into a sprawl of housing tracts, office parks, and shopping centers.

The trio of communities was known collectively as New King City because that's where the tech companies were, the new economic engine of the city, and where all the young, educated, and well-off families lived.

Until a couple of weeks ago, it was where Wade lived too, along with the majority of King City cops. The schools were better, the grass was greener, the skies were bluer, the smiles were brighter, and the streets were safer. Or maybe it just seemed that way because everything was so new and you were never more than ten yards away from a Jamba Juice.

He used to pass this Denny's sign on his morning commute, a landmark telling him that he was ten minutes from seeing the river and the downtown skyline and twenty minutes from pulling into his parking spot at One King Plaza, depending on the congestion on the bridge.

Now the Denny's sign marked home.

He made a conscious effort not to look at the newspaper kiosks outside the restaurant door. The corruption story was still playing out on the front page even though the major plot twists, revelations, and denouement were past. Reading about it all now was like watching a TV series based on a hit movie that had already produced three crappy sequels that nobody liked.

The moment he stepped inside the restaurant, everybody became self-conscious and awkward. He was used to it. All uniformed cops were.

Even law-abiding citizens felt guilty of something with a cop in the room; as if they were afraid that he could read their darkest thoughts or that they might be seized by a sudden, uncontrollable urge to commit a major felony.

In his experience, only children greeted the sight of a police officer with enthusiasm and pleasure. Children like order and security. Most adults do too, but those feelings are complicated by issues of ego, dominance, control, status, and sex, all of which come bubbling up from the bog of the unconscious when you are confronted with a man with the power to take your freedom or your life.

Wade took a booth facing the cash register and the front door on the remote chance that the place got held up while he was eating.

A waitress slouched beside his table, poured him a cup of coffee, and offered him a laminated menu. She'd waited on him before. She was laminated in the transparent bitterness and disappointment that had coated her for thirty years.

He ordered a Grand Slam breakfast with scrambled eggs so he wouldn't dribble any yolk on his uniform. She snatched up the menu and walked away.

While he waited for his breakfast, he opened up his briefcase and took out the files on the two officers who'd be working under his command.

The chief had given him a choice yesterday in the park—he could quit or he could take the assignment and get killed. Either way, Wade got fucked over and the department won.

He took the reassignment without protest, even though he was well aware of what the chief was doing.

The way Wade looked at it, cops are supposed to go to dangerous neighborhoods and make them safe.

If he was unwilling to do that, he shouldn't have become a cop to start with.

He'd put off reading the two personnel files until breakfast because he knew that he'd be stuck with what the chief considered the dregs of the department, the fools, the addicts, the pariahs, the cops that no other cops could stand.

Cops like him.

He opened the first file.

Billy Hagen, twenty-two, the lowest scoring officer among the new class at the police academy. A rookie. He grew up in the north end, in one of the old row-house neighborhoods. His parents were divorced, mother worked as a waitress, father was a mechanic. He barely graduated from high school and, judging by his transcripts, he had bluffed his way through community college too. Billy's last job before becoming a cop was at Best Buy, selling electronics.

The only reason Billy made the cut was because the department was desperate for new manpower. Considering that the pay was awful, the benefits were pitiful, the risk of bodily harm was high, and nobody trusted or respected cops anymore, they couldn't be too picky.

Wade studied Billy Hagen's picture. The kid was blond haired and fresh faced and had a cocky, mischievous smile.

He'd probably get Wade killed if he didn't get himself killed first. Still, a rookie was better than getting a drunk who'd been on the job for twenty years. Hagen was too inexperienced to have picked up any bad habits yet. The challenge for Wade would be keeping Hagen alive long enough to learn something.

The waitress dropped his plate of eggs, bacon, hash browns, and toast in front of him, freshened his coffee, and dragged her ass away.

Wade closed Hagen's file and opened the next one, which he perused as he ate.

Charlotte Greene, twenty-four, African-American, top of her class at the academy. Another rookie. She grew up in a nice housing tract in New King City about a mile away from his house. Her father was a shrink and her mother was a lawyer. Professional liberals, Wade decided. She was a straight-A student in high school and graduated with a bachelor's degree in sociology from the state university.

Obviously, Charlotte Greene wanted to reform society and rescue the oppressed and was talked into thinking a badge was the way to do it.

Since African-Americans made up less than 3 percent of the King City population, and even fewer were high school graduates, it was clear to Wade that she'd been recruited as part of the halfhearted public relations effort to diversify the department with women and people of color and create some positive press in the wake of the corruption scandal.

But this was a reform that was doomed to failure. Chief Reardon was a conservative bigot who believed women were biologically incapable of police work and that having a skin color other than Caucasian was probable cause for arrest.

She was too smart, too liberal, and too black to be a King City cop. And she wasn't going to be very happy when she discovered that for herself.

Wade knew she'd fight him on everything. Maybe that was a good thing too. Her anger and tenacity would help her survive.

He motioned to the waitress for his check, put the files in his briefcase, and closed it. He had one day to get settled in before his officers showed up for work.

Three experienced officers weren't enough to man an outpost in a violent neighborhood like Darwin Gardens. But he was going in with two rookies.

The assignment was meant to be a death sentence for him. Maybe he deserved it, but Hagen and Greene certainly didn't. He'd have to find a way to protect them.

The waitress approached the table.

"It's on the house," she said.

This was how the rot started, with little gratuities like that, until you thought you were entitled to them and much more.

"I appreciate the gesture," Wade said. "But I'd prefer to pay."

She shook her head. "We never charge the police. It's our policy."

"You charged me yesterday," he said.

"I didn't know you were a cop."

"Pretend that you still don't."

"I haven't got much of an imagination," she said, turned her back to him, and went on to take another customer's order.

He didn't understand why she fought him. It would have taken far less effort to just accept his money. And she looked like someone who'd given up on making any effort years ago.

Wade left enough cash on the table to cover his bill, the tax, and a tip and walked out.

CHAPTER FOUR

He drove west toward downtown in his five-year-old Mustang, one of the dark-green, special-edition fastbacks that Ford made to cash in on memories of the iconic car that Steve McQueen drove in *Bullitt.*

The car was a surprise thirty-sixth-birthday present to Wade from his wife, the breadwinner in the house. She worked in an advertising agency. Making deodorant seem sexy, glamorous, and exciting paid a lot more than arresting drug dealers.

He liked the 5-speed, manual transmission and the 315-horsepower, 4.6-liter, 24-valve V-8 engine that redlined at 6,500 rpm and could hit 150 miles per hour.

He hated everything else about it, particularly the gunsight *Bullitt* logo embossed on the steering wheel, the metal sill plates, and the ridiculous fake gas cap glued on the back of the car.

Wade told Alison that he loved the car, of course. That was a husband's duty. And Wade always did his duty.

But what he was really thinking was that if she thought he'd like the car from *Bullitt*, that's what she should have bought him—a 1968 Mustang GT fastback—not a new Mustang adorned with a lot of useless plastic garbage.

This was a muscle car designed for middle-aged men who never had any muscles of their own, who thought Neil Diamond was edgy, and who were trying to gather the courage to ask their doctors for Viagra.

So he kept it in the garage as much as possible, never listened to Neil Diamond when he drove it, and used a police vehicle whenever possible.

Now that Alison had thrown him out of the house, Wade wanted to pry all that fake Hollywood crap off the car so he'd be left with just a green Mustang. He didn't do it because he was afraid that his thirteen-year-old daughter, Brooke, would take it as an act of rage directed at her mother.

Maybe it would be.

He took the curving off-ramp to the King's Crossing Bridge and unconsciously sat up to take in the postcard view of the suspension bridge, the river, and the downtown skyline set against the jagged West Hills.

The clump of office buildings that was downtown King City wasn't that distinctive or memorable. It was the King's Crossing and the five other bridges that spanned the Chewelah River that gave the city its character. And the very best view of them was from the King's Crossing Bridge, the highest of the bunch.

At least once a week, traffic on the King's Crossing would snarl to a standstill because some jerk slowed down to look at the view, crashed into another car, and caused a multicar pileup.

Wade had seen the bridges countless times but always took a glance north and south anyway. Each bridge was unique, a perfect example of a particular kind of engineering, and built from steel and iron mined from the West Hills.

The bridges seemed imbued with the ambition, the daring, and the tenacity that got them made. He found something comforting and invigorating about the sight.

But once he crossed into downtown, the magic was gone. The bridge spilled him right into One King Plaza, the government center, which was dominated by the stone castle that was the original city hall and a symbol of excess and ego.

King City grew quickly after it was founded, thriving on the abundant natural resources, the railroad, and commerce on the river.

By the turn of the century, the city stretched over both sides of the river. It had smoothly transitioned from a largely agricultural-based economy into an industrial center. Steel mills, lumberyards, breweries, and various manufacturing plants lined the shores, pumping smoke into the air day and night.

But by the turn of the next century, the city's economy was in shambles. The mines were either depleted or too costly to keep in operation. The forests and farmland had all been subdivided and developed. The steel, lumber, and other major industries had moved overseas. The Chewelah River was no longer a primary means of moving goods, and its water was so toxic that even fish couldn't live in it.

Now the docks, railroad yards, factories, and warehouses sat vacant and rotting under the sunbaked, brown haze, the decay spreading to the forgotten, crime-ridden neighborhoods around them that were once the city's safest and most prosperous places to live.

That's where Wade was going, to Division Street, once the central shopping district of the south side, the area now known as Darwin Gardens.

It was only four miles from One King Plaza and a world away.

The buildings on both sides of Division Street were two or three stories tall, the kind of Edwardian stone, brick, and concrete buildings found on any Main Street in small-town America. Now they looked like abandoned jails, iron bars over the windows and doors, water-stained plywood mounted where there had once been glass. Everything was shades of gray, all the color eroded away by time and neglect.

Homeless men and women huddled in the doorways and alcoves with their belongings in bulging Hefty bags piled high in rusted grocery carts. They glared out at him from the shadows like owls.

There were still a few businesses in operation on the street, all with barred windows—a barber shop, a mini-mart, a psychic, a shoe-repair place, and a check-cashing operation.

Three hookers stood listlessly in front of the check-cashing place, hoping to get a share of somebody's paycheck before the mini-mart did. Or maybe they worked for the check casher, who was looking for a way to get some of his cash back before it got too far out the door. Maybe it was both of those things.

An Escalade, clad in sheets of after-market chrome, cruised by in the opposite direction, the driver slowing down to get a good look at Wade.

The driver was a Native American man, maybe in his twenties, wearing a tank top that showed off his prison-yard muscles and his tats. His eyes had a cold, sharklike flatness that must have taken a lot of practice in front of a mirror to achieve.

The Escalade moved on and so did Wade.

The new police substation was on the corner of Division Street and Arness Avenue in a storefront that had most recently been occupied by an X-rated video business. The sign for "Red Hot XXX-Treme Video" was still above the door.

Wade cruised past the two-story brick building slowly. If he squinted, he could see the words "King City Police Substation," which had recently been etched in small gold lettering on the glass front door, right above a DVD return slot under the words, in big white letters, "Was It Good for You? Cum Again."

He drove around the corner onto Arness.

Behind the building, a new cyclone fence topped with razor wire enclosed a small parking lot where three dented, scratched, and dirt-covered Crown Vic black-and-white cruisers were parked side by side. There was a pile of broken DVD shelving beside an overflowing Dumpster. Some of it looked burned. A thick chain and huge padlock secured the gate.

Wade made a U-turn and pulled up in front of the storefront and behind an old Buick that was molting oxidized paint.

A pear-shaped man who looked to be in his fifties emerged from the Buick. He wore a cap from a factory that had closed down fifteen years ago and had a cigar stub in his mouth that looked like he'd been chewing on it just as long. There was a retractable key ring with a few hundred keys on it clipped to his belt, weighing down his pants below his gelatinous belly, which was barely covered by an untucked, oversized aloha shirt.

Wade got out and met him on the sidewalk.

"Mr. Claggett? I'm Tom Wade." He offered his hand, but Claggett didn't take it.

"It's one thing to rent my place to the cops—everybody understands you've got to make a buck—but it's another if they think we're buddies."

Wade looked past Claggett to the street. The Escalade had made a U-turn and was idling at the next corner, the driver watching them. So were the hookers. Even the homeless people were peering cautiously out of their alcoves.

"Would you prefer that the police weren't here?"

"Doesn't matter what I think. You're not staying, anyway," Claggett said, going to the door. His keys jingled as he walked. "It's a publicity stunt."

"Do you see any reporters around?"

"It's safer for them to read the press release than to come down here." Claggett took his key chain, fumbled around until he found the right key, unlocked the iron grate, folded it aside, then unlocked the door. "Besides, the city only signed a ninety-day lease. What more do I need to know?"

"You don't know me," Wade said and surveyed his new command.

The DVD racks were gone, but the walls were decorated with posters advertising movies like *Asscrack Bandits 4*, *Cum Cannon 23*, and *Titfuckers on Parade*. But that's not what caught Wade's attention. There was a scorched section of the wall near the window, burned clear through to the framing, the two-by-fours charred black.

"What happened here?" Wade asked, walking over to study the damage. The linoleum below the window was curled up and bubbled from the fire, and the ceiling had black streaks where it was licked by flames. The fire had burned hot and died fast.

"The previous tenant had an accident."

"I guess those movies really were red-hot," Wade said.

"*Titfuckers on Parade* is pretty good," Claggett said.

"What did the fire department say?"

"I don't know if they've seen it," Claggett said.

"About the fire," Wade said.

"Nobody asked them. The tenant put it out with a fire extinguisher."

"What did the insurance company say?"

Claggett snorted and waved off the comment. "The damage doesn't come close to meeting my deductible. My rates are high enough as it is without getting them jacked up by filing a claim."

Wade glanced at the damage. His guess was that someone had tossed a Molotov cocktail through the window. The fire would have been much worse if the bottle hadn't broken against the bars on its way in.

"Do people here have a big problem with porn?"

Claggett laughed but managed to keep his cigar stub clamped between his lips.

"Only that they can't get enough of it."

That's what Wade thought.

"Why didn't you repair the wall?"

"The tenant moved out right after the accident and then you moved in. No one said anything about it and the lease agreement is signed, so now it's your problem. You could cover it with one of those posters."

Wade shifted his gaze to the rest of the place.

A chipped and beaten Formica-topped counter ran across almost the entire width of the room, creating a partition. Wade guessed it was probably repurposed from the video store. A gate made of unpainted wood bridged the remaining distance between the counter and the wall.

Behind the counter were four gunmetal gray desks and chairs, like those found at police stations all over the city. Atop the desks were computers from the Paleolithic era of computing, phones, an old microwave, lamps, boxes of office supplies, and other equipment that nobody had bothered to unpack, set up, or organize. Some file cabinets, a refrigerator, a microwave, and four gym lockers were crammed together in a corner along with more unopened boxes and crates. There was a gun locker mounted and locked on the wall. The chief had tossed Wade the key to the gun locker that day in the park.

Wade walked through the gate and between the desks to the back of the station, where three holding cells had been built. The doors were made of thick iron mesh, and each cell contained a concrete block for a cot and a stainless steel toilet/sink combination.

All the construction work that had been done to transform the video store into an adequate police substation was cosmetically unfinished and raw. No primer or paint had been applied to any of it.

"You're responsible for paint and improvements," Claggett said, reading Wade's sour expression. "I just provide the four walls and the roof."

"There's a big hole in the wall," Wade said, gesturing to the fire damage.

"I didn't say the walls and the roof would be solid," Claggett said. "Just that they'd be there. Are your friends coming back to finish up?"

"I don't think so," Wade said.

Claggett looked at him. "Can I ask you a personal question, Officer?"

"Go ahead," he said.

"What did you do wrong to end up here?"

"My job," Wade said.

"Maybe you're in the wrong job."

"Or I'm in the right job with the wrong people."

"You're pretty sure of yourself."

"That's what they tell me," Wade said.

"Or you're a damn fool."

"They tell me that too."

"So which is it?"

"Could be they're the same thing." Across the room Wade saw a door that was ajar, revealing a staircase beyond it. "What's upstairs?"

"An apartment nobody wants," Claggett said. "Tenants down here usually use it as storage space."

"I'd like to see it," Wade said.

Claggett led him through the door and up the stairs. He unlocked the door and held it open for Wade, who walked past him into the apartment.

There was a kitchenette without appliances, a living area, and a separate bedroom and bath. The carpet throughout was filthy and stained. The walls had a piss-yellow, weathered tinge from age and sun damage. The barred windows in the bedroom and living room overlooked Division Street.

A cell with a view.

Wade went to one corner of the living room, crouched, and pulled up the edge of the carpet to expose the hardwood floor underneath. With a little work, it would clean up nice. All the walls needed were a coat of white paint.

He stood up again. "I'll take it."

"You've already got it. It comes with the space downstairs."

"I want to rent it for myself as a place to live."

"You *want* to live here?" Claggett asked, incredulous.

"How does seven hundred and fifty dollars a month sound to you?"

"But you could stay up here for nothing," Claggett said.

"You're not much of a businessman," Wade said. "Do you have a problem with making money?"

"I'm out of practice. I don't get the opportunity very often."

"Bring me a rental agreement to sign."

"You want it made out for week to week?"

"Month to month," Wade said. "I'll pay you the first and last in advance."

"Do you really think you're going to be here that long?"

"I'm optimistic," Wade said.

"You're fucking nuts," Claggett said.

CHAPTER FIVE

They went back downstairs. Claggett gave Wade a set of keys to all the doors and locks in and around the building and then hurried out.

Wade found the keys to the squad cars on one of the desks and went out back to his fenced-in parking lot to inspect his fleet.

The first squad car was filled with trash, as if someone had emptied a few neighborhood garbage cans into it. Amid the papers, cans, and bottles, he saw soiled diapers, rotting food, and even a dead bird. The upholstery in the front seat was patched with filthy duct tape. He glanced at the odometer—a mere 287,000 miles.

The second car had about the same number of miles on the odometer as the first one but wasn't filled with trash. The molded plastic backseats and floor were coated with dried vomit and feces instead.

The third car was practically new, with just 215,000 miles on the engine, but the interior looked and smelled as if the entire police department had used it as a urinal and then invited a few stray dogs to relieve themselves in it too.

He walked around the cars and checked the tires. They were inflated and the treads were in pretty good shape. Anything above bald was better than he'd expected.

Wade popped the hoods and opened the trunks on all three cars.

The engines seemed intact and the vehicles were stocked with crime scene kits, first aid kits, and all the other necessary equipment.

They'd even given him radar guns. He wasn't planning on writing any speeding tickets. That would just piss people off. He had bigger problems to deal with.

The cars were old, beaten up, and purposely filled with filth by his fellow cops as a not-so-subtle message to him about how enthused they were to have him back. But the vehicles seemed to be in basic working condition. That was good enough for him.

He closed the hoods and the trunks, locked up the cars, and went back inside.

Wade spent the next few hours doing a thorough inventory of the equipment, weapons, ammunition, and office supplies that had been left for him. To his surprise, he found everything that was needed for the proper operation of the substation.

He knew the department hadn't done it out of concern for his safety or for the good of the community. It was about limiting the blowback. The chief wanted to be sure that when Wade or his two officers got seriously injured or killed that the bloodshed couldn't be blamed on substandard or missing equipment.

With the inventory done, Wade unpacked and organized his station. He arranged the desks and made sure that all the computer terminals were linked to the police network, which utilized the cable lines that were strung up on telephone poles all over the old part of King City. It wasn't the best system. A couple of years ago, a runaway trash truck knocked over a pole and shut down the police communications network for hours.

Wade double-checked that the radios were hooked up to the dispatcher, which they were, though he didn't expect to be sent out on many calls. People in Darwin Gardens didn't call the police when they needed help.

Not yet, anyway.

It was late afternoon by the time he finished setting things up. There was still a lot of cosmetic work to do in the station, mostly patching and painting, but all of that could wait. The important thing was that the station was functional and ready for the arrival in the morning of his two rookie officers.

But he wasn't quite ready for them yet. He sat down at one of the desks, took out a legal pad, and gave some serious thought to the shift schedule.

Ordinarily, patrol shifts were broken down into three eight-hour chunks.

He knew from experience that the day shift, 8:00 a.m. to 4:00 p.m., was when most of the nonviolent crimes occurred, like shoplifting, check forgery, and minor domestic squabbles.

From 4:00 p.m. to midnight was when most of the crimes-in-progress calls came in and officers had to deal with burglaries, carjackings, and robberies.

The graveyard shift, from midnight to 8:00 a.m., was aptly named. It wasn't just the dead of night—it was also when most of the rapes, drive-by shootings, drunk-driving accidents, overdoses, and murders occurred. The bloodshed was especially heavy between 10:00 p.m. and 2:00 a.m., so sometimes a fourth shift was added from 8:00 p.m. to 4:00 a.m. to put more officers on the streets.

But Wade didn't have the manpower for that. He barely had the manpower for three shifts, since he wasn't ready to trust his rookies alone. They were coming to him with four hundred hours of field training, but it wasn't done down here.

Rookies usually got stuck with the graveyard shift, the long nights of blood and vomit, while the senior officers got the easier days and the good nights' sleep and family face time that came with it.

The problem with the day shift was that the brass, the bureaucrats, the press, the politicians, and the special-interest groups were awake too, and looking over your shoulder, which could be worse than dealing with rapists, drunks, and cold-blooded murderers.

That was one problem Wade wouldn't have. He sketched out a shift schedule for the first few weeks that involved each of them taking twelve-hour shifts. Greene and Hagen weren't going to like it, but they could take some satisfaction that the schedule would be a lot more brutal on him. He couldn't send them out alone yet, not during the deadliest hours, so to be there with them, he'd allotted himself only five hours of sleep a night.

It was a good thing his commute home would be just two flights of stairs.

His stomach growled loudly enough to startle him, and he realized that he'd worked right through lunch and nearly to dinner. It was time to venture out into the community for some meat, which he considered the one essential element of any satisfying meal. He'd eat a salad as long as there were chunks of meat in it somewhere.

Wade stepped outside, locked the door, slid the steel grate shut, and locked it too. It was warm and still, as if the air itself were hesitating.

He turned around and carefully surveyed the street, mindful that he presented an attractive target.

Not a lot had changed since morning.

A few more hookers milled around in front of the check-cashing place to his right on the northeast corner of Division Street and Weaver Street. They were out foraging for clients. There weren't as many homeless around. They were out foraging for food and drinks.

The Escalade was gone, but there were half a dozen sullen-faced, tattooed young men huddled in front of the mini-mart directly across the street, watching him.

They wore bright-red bandanas or baseball caps turned backward, bright-white running shoes, sports team jerseys, and oversize pants that drooped off their asses to flash their boxers. Menace radiated off them like heat. He could almost see it shimmering from their skin, but he didn't sense imminent danger.

Wade glanced to his left. There was a fifties-era coffee shop on the southwest corner of Division and Arness that had floor-to-ceiling windows all the way around. It had a red, sweeping roofline that seemed to soar off into the air, where its sharply pointed edge pierced a starburst-shaped sign that read "Pancake Galaxy."

There was a buoyant optimism and wacky exuberance inherent in the space-age design that endured despite the decay, the desperation, and the poverty of the surrounding neighborhood. But that enthusiasm was expressed in more than the dramatic, accelerating architecture—it was the only building on the street without bars over the windows. That told him something about the people who owned the restaurant and how they were viewed by the neighborhood.

Wade looked both ways, crossed the intersection to the restaurant, and went inside.

The restaurant was like a museum exhibit of the 1950s, futuristic modernism. Free-form boomerang- and amoeba-shaped counters and architectural accents were set against a dizzying mix of surface materials: Formica, brick, stainless steel, lava rock, and ceramic tiles. The red vinyl bar stools were cantilevered away from the counters and over the terrazzo floors so they almost seemed to be floating. Enormous white globes of light hung from the ceiling like planets and made the silver flecks on the counter-tops sparkle like stardust.

There were framed illustrations everywhere of a happy-faced cartoon pancake with arms and legs. In each picture, the smiling pancake was dressed as something different—a pirate, an astronaut, a lumberjack, a doctor, a firefighter, an Indian, a football player, a chef, a scuba diver, a pope. He was a pancake for all people, all countries, and all seasons.

An emaciated hooker in latex hot pants and a loose-fitting tank top sat alone at a table, holding a stack of pancakes in her hands and eating it like a sandwich. She kept her eyes on him as she ate, oblivious to the dab of butter she'd put on the tip of her nose.

There was an old man wearing an emerald-blue Members Only jacket, cargo pants, and glasses with lenses the size of computer monitors sharing a booth with a woman whose sparse hair was puffed out into a dandelion do. They froze to look at him, the man as he lifted a coffee cup to his mouth, the woman as she stuffed a wad of Kleenex into her abundant cleavage.

A gaunt man with sunken cheeks and big owl eyes sat on a stool behind the cash register. He was well into his social security years and wearing a flannel shirt that seemed to be two sizes too big for him. He had a thin plastic tube under his nostrils that ran over his ears and down to an oxygen tank that was on wheels beside him. A curl of smoke rose from a cigarette in an ashtray on the counter.

"You know you're not supposed to smoke around an oxygen tank," Wade said.

"What do you care?" the man asked. His voice sounded like it was clawing its way through gravel.

"You might blow the place up, and I hadn't planned on this being my last meal."

"You never can tell," the man said. "Especially down here."

Wade took a seat at the counter, as far away from the cashier as he could get. The waitress approached and handed him a laminated menu.

She was in her late twenties and wore faded jeans and a loose, short-sleeve blouse that was open one button more than it probably should have been, a dream-catcher necklace drawing his eye to her chest. She had black hair tied back in a ponytail and a ballerina's body, thin but strong, her skin an almost edible caramel.

"Don't worry about Dad. He wouldn't dare blow the place up until everybody has settled their checks," she said, offering Wade her hand. "I'm Amanda. My friends call me Mandy."

"Tom Wade," he said, shaking her hand. He glanced back at her father, who was stealing a drag on his cigarette and couldn't have been any whiter if he were chalk. Mandy didn't get her Indian blood from him.

Mandy followed his gaze. "That warm, cuddly character is my father, Peter Guthrie, the inspiration for Peter Pancake." She tapped the menu and the smiling pancake on the front cover.

"I see the resemblance," Wade said.

"What can I get you, Officer?" she asked as she picked up a clear-glass coffeepot and filled the thick white mug in front of him.

"Call me Tom. I'd like a short stack of pancakes and a side of bacon—soft, not crispy, please."

Mandy walked back into the open kitchen and tied on an apron. "I would have figured you for a crispy man, Tom."

"Are you going to be disappointed if I put sugar in my coffee?"

"I won't be disappointed but I'll be surprised," she said as she poured batter into a pan and laid some strips of bacon on the flat grill. The bacon sizzled instantly. "You strike me as a man who takes the bitterness as it comes and doesn't try to sweeten things up."

"You got all that from me already?"

"You're not a hard man to read," she said. "I watched you as you walked over here. It's in your stride and in the way you wear your uniform. They call it body language for a reason."

He thought about what she'd said. She'd been watching his body and how it moved.

Was she attracted to him?

It had been a long time since he'd asked himself that question about a woman or cared about the answer.

"And mine says crispy bacon and black coffee," he said.

"It does to me," Mandy said. "But I was only half right."

"Can I ask you a question?"

"Sure, Tom," she replied in a jaunty sort of way, like saying his name amused her. There was something of a tease in it too.

He liked it.

"Why don't you have bars on your windows like everybody else?"

"If I wanted to live in a prison, I'd rob somebody," Peter Guthrie answered for her in a rasp that soon gave way to a coughing jag.

"My mom and dad opened this restaurant forty-nine years ago," Mandy said. "Not much else has lasted here. So we're, like, on hallowed ground."

"Everybody is welcome as long as they behave themselves," Guthrie choked out between coughs.

"What happens if they don't?"

"I've got Old Betty," Guthrie said. Wade turned to see the old man lifting a sawed-off shotgun from its hiding place behind the counter. "This will cut a man in half."

"You know it for a fact," Wade said and wondered how long ago Guthrie had found that out for himself.

That's when Mandy came out of the kitchen holding a plate in each hand. She laid them down in front of Wade.

The six buttermilk pancakes were hot, fluffy, and huge, with a ball of butter nearly as large as a scoop of ice cream melting on top. And this was the short stack. But he wasn't going to complain. The six strips of bacon were thick and meaty and had a smoky aroma.

Wade was practically salivating as he tucked a napkin under his collar. "You should serve this with a side of Lipitor."

"Would you like some maple syrup with that?"

"What does my body language tell you?"

She poured syrup on the pancakes for him and set the bottle down next to his plate. "You respect tradition. Pancakes and maple syrup go together, so that's how you'll take it. Besides, you wouldn't have put on that napkin if you weren't afraid of dripping on yourself."

"You should have been a detective," he said.

Wade took a bite of his pancakes. They were the best that he'd ever had, thick with buttermilk and yet so light they were like flavored air. The maple syrup was sticky sweet and natural; he could almost taste the bark that the sap had bled through. He quickly had another bite.

"How about you?" she asked.

"Been there," he said. "Done that."

"Is that why you're here?"

"Don't you already know the answer to that question?"

"There are limits to how much you can learn from studying someone's body language."

He did some studying of his own, looking for signs of insincerity in her expression. What he saw was a woman who was relaxed and amused, in no hurry to do anything else but stand there talking to him. "Don't you read the paper or watch the news?"

"I've been away for a while and I've been preoccupied since I got back. Are you somebody I should know?"

"I hope so," he said, instantly regretting his words and hoping she wouldn't take them as a suggestive come-on.

Then again, he thought, *maybe it wouldn't be so bad if she did.*

Before he could find out one way or another, he heard the sound of breaking glass, followed by whoops, hollers, and loud metallic thunks coming from outside.

Mandy looked past him to the street, her smile doing a fast fade, her entire body tensing up. Her father reached for Old Betty.

Wade took another bite of his pancakes, swiveled in his seat, and looked outside.

The gang of men who'd been standing across the street from the station before was now gathered around his Mustang, attacking it with tire irons and crowbars.

CHAPTER SIX

Wade didn't really care about the Mustang. He'd fantasized about trashing it himself several times. What he wanted to do was finish his pancakes, resume the light banter, and send the gang a thank-you note, but he knew that wouldn't help establish his authority in the neighborhood.

This was a direct challenge that had to be met with a strong response, or he might as well turn in his badge.

Wade reluctantly pulled off his napkin and dabbed his lips with it.

"Excuse me for a minute," he said and got up from his seat.

Mandy looked at him incredulously. "You're not going out there, are you?" He nodded. "Aren't you going to wait for backup?"

It was pointless to call for help, and he knew it. If any cops actually came, it would only be so they could watch on the sidelines and cheer his opponents on.

This was exactly the kind of confrontation the department was hoping for when they'd banished him here. He didn't need them here to see it.

"I'm all there is," Wade said and headed toward the door.

"Do you mind paying before you go?" Guthrie asked.

Wade turned and gave him a look. "You don't think I'll be coming back?"

"I ask everybody to pay before they leave the restaurant," Guthrie said. "Especially the customers who are likely to get gunned down in the street."

Wade took out his wallet, picked out a ten-dollar bill, and handed it to him. "Thanks for the vote of confidence."

"I'm a pragmatist," Guthrie said.

"So am I," Wade said.

"Pragmatists are survivors," he said.

"I hope you're right." Wade walked outside.

The gang was still taking swings at his car with their tire irons as he strode casually into the intersection. They saw him coming and looked to the Escalade parked up the street for guidance. They got some kind of signal from the shark-eyed Indian in the driver's seat and resumed trashing the car, looking at Wade defiantly as they did it.

Wade drew his gun and fired four shots in rapid succession at the Escalade, blowing out the two front tires and putting two bullets into the front grill.

The Escalade slumped forward on its haunches and hissed like a wounded bull.

The gunshots were still echoing in the air when the driver's-side door flew open and the Indian jumped out. There was a gun in his hand, which he held down at his side. His muscled arms and shoulders were covered with elaborate, interwoven tattoos.

There was a loud clatter as the six men around Wade's Mustang dropped their tire irons and crowbars and drew their guns.

But Wade kept his attention on the Indian. The others wouldn't do anything without the nod from him.

The Indian looked at his flat tire, then walked around to the front of his Escalade to examine the perforated grill, an aftermarket piece of chrome mesh that must have cost a lot. It was ruined now.

The Indian turned and faced Wade.

"You killed my car," the Indian said, his lips drawn into a snarl, giving him a furious glare.

The expression was scary looking, but it seemed to Wade as if it were meant more for an audience than for any one individual. The glare might have made other people wet themselves, but the theatricality of it diminished any impact it might have had on Wade.

"Guess that makes us even," Wade said.

"You're a fucking dead man," the Indian said, the gun still held loosely at his side, but his arm twitched as he wrestled with the decision of whether or not to start firing.

"My advice to you is to drop the gun and walk away," Wade said.

"There's one of you and seven of us," the Indian said.

Wade shook his head. "It's only five."

"How do you figure that?"

"Because if you and your friends don't drop your weapons by the count of three, I'll shoot you in the head and then I'll kill the guy with the loose pants."

The men at Wade's car traded looks among themselves.

"Which one of us is that?" one of them asked.

Wade didn't turn to see who had spoken. He kept his gaze locked on the Indian.

"You're full of shit," the Indian said.

"One," Wade said.

The Indian looked Wade in the eye. What he saw there wasn't confidence or bravery or a willingness to die. What he saw was that a decision had been made. He saw rectitude.

Or all he saw was a reflection of his own doubts.

"Two," Wade said.

The Indian dropped his gun. Wade kept his gun on him and glanced at the men by his car.

"Three," he said.

They dropped their weapons too, following the Indian's lead. But Wade also saw relief on their faces.

Wade shifted his gaze back to the Indian, who was snarling. It seemed like a much more natural expression for him than the last one. He thought about telling him but decided the Indian wouldn't appreciate the observation.

"This isn't over." The Indian raised his right hand, made a gun with his fingers, and mimed firing it at him.

"You know where to find me." Wade tipped his head toward the station but kept his gun aimed at the Indian. "Stop by anytime and we can discuss it."

The Indian walked away and the others followed him, leaving their guns and crowbars on the sidewalk.

He watched them until they rounded the corner of the block and disappeared from sight.

Wade holstered his weapon and immediately broke into a full-body sweat. He knew that he'd narrowly escaped execution and that it was just a dry run for what was to come.

But next time, he wouldn't be facing them alone. He'd have Officers Charlotte Greene and Billy Hagen watching his back.

Maybe that wasn't such a good thing.

Maybe they'd simply end up adding their own corpses to the eventual body count. Their own. He wasn't sure he wanted that on his conscience.

Wade picked up the Indian's gun by sticking a ballpoint pen in the barrel and went over to his car to inspect the damage. It looked even worse up close. The body was covered with deep dents, gouges, and scratches. All the lights and windows were broken, the plastic front grill was smashed in, and the seats were coated with a layer of glass pebbles.

And yet somehow the fake gas cap with the *Bullitt* logo on it had come through the assault untouched.

He set down the Indian's gun, picked up a tire iron from the sidewalk, and pried the cap off with one quick jerk. The cheap plastic broke apart and flew into the street.

When Wade looked up again, he saw Mandy standing outside of the restaurant staring at him, her arms folded under her chest. Her father came out behind her, wheeling his oxygen tank. The hookers and homeless and a lot of other people were stepping out of doorways and peering out between the bars of their windows to see what would happen next.

Hefting the tire iron, Wade strode across the street to the Escalade and took a swing at the windshield. The laminated glass radiated with cracks. He continued to swing at it until the windshield crumpled and caved in on the dashboard.

Wade walked around the car, smashing the windows as he went and busting the taillights. When he got to the front of the Escalade, he broke the headlights, caved in the shot-up grill, and took a few more whacks at the hood for good measure before he threw the tire iron into the SUV and walked back to his Mustang.

He opened the dented trunk, the metal groaning as he lifted it, and then opened his gun locker, which resembled an ice chest. He put on rubber gloves, gathered up the discarded guns from the street, and dumped them in the locker. Then he peeled off his rubber gloves, tossed them in the trunk, and closed the lid, which he had to slam shut twice before it stuck.

Wade put his right hand on his holstered gun and strode into the open intersection again, looking in all directions for a possible shooter as he headed back to the restaurant to finish his meal.

As he got up close to Mandy, the look on her face and the way she stood asked a question, but he didn't know whether it was intended for him or for her to answer.

So he just said what was on his mind. "I hope my pancakes haven't gotten too cold."

Wade passed Mandy and her father and went into the restaurant.

CHAPTER SEVEN

When Wade was facing down the Indian, he wasn't really thinking about the situation. He was thinking about his father.

Glenn Wade wasn't an imposing man, but he had strength. It wasn't muscle; it was something in his eyes and in his bearing. His skin was dark and lined from a lifetime of living, working, and playing outdoors. He was a man who would've looked natural wearing a cowboy hat, but he wouldn't have felt natural doing it. He would have felt ridiculous.

During the spring and summer, Glenn ran Granite Cove Park, the Loon Lake campground and resort that his grandfather built fifty miles north of King City and two miles west off the highway to Canada.

Granite Cove consisted of four red cabins, a general store, a boat dock, a camping area, and the two-story house that the Wade family lived in year-round.

Wade's parents worked full time at the resort throughout the spring and summer. He and his younger sister, Elizabeth, helped out after school and throughout their summer vacations.

During the late fall and winter, when the resort was closed for the season, Glenn Wade worked full time as a deputy sheriff, one of only a handful enforcing the law on the lake and the surrounding community. He was a deputy during the summer too, but only part time. Since the resort and the boat dock were such a big part of the local economy, it was more important to the community to have him running the place than to have him out on patrol. But he was on call 24-7 if something came up.

Once in a while, Wade rode with his father in his patrol car or in his patrol boat, which was actually just their fishing boat with a county flag on the stern and a bullhorn under the bench. They didn't talk about much during those ride-alongs, and that was fine with Wade. It was time alone with his dad that didn't involve washing the boats, patching roofs, cleaning toilets, or raking the beach.

On one such night, when Wade was twelve years old, they were driving the pitch-black roads around the lake, keeping an eye on the empty lake houses, making sure nobody busted into them during the off-season, though it happened a lot anyway despite the patrol. There was too much lake, and too many houses, for Glenn to maintain a vigil on them all.

It hadn't started snowing yet, but it was cold enough outside at night to keep a milk shake from melting. Wade and his sister had tried it. The darker it was at night, the colder it seemed to be. He could almost measure the temperature by staring into the darkness.

A call came in from the dispatcher in Silverton. The cook at the roadhouse and bait shack on Highway 99 was frantic. Four guys from the lumber mill were drinking their paychecks, beating up on the waitress, and trashing the place.

Glenn got there in about five minutes. They drove up to the clapboard roadhouse just as a chair flew through a window and landed in front of the two pickup trucks in the gravel parking lot.

Through the broken window, Wade could see the four men inside the restaurant. They were drunk, rowdy, and spoiling for a fight. If there'd been any other customers that night, they were long gone now.

His father parked the car beside the two pickup trucks, took the gun out of his holster, and placed it in the glove box, slamming the lid shut.

"No matter what happens, you stay right here," his father told him.

"You're going up against them without your gun?"

"I don't want anybody to die tonight," Glenn said. "Guns tend to bring out the death in a room."

"But there's four of them," Wade said. "How are you going to protect yourself?"

"Most of the time, it's not whether or not you have a gun in your hand that matters," his father said. "It's what you stand for and how strong you stand for it."

That wasn't the first time Wade had heard that "what you stand for" line from his dad. It was his father's all-purpose explanation for every decision he made on any subject, whether it was whom he voted for, how much he'd pay for a shirt, or which kind of bait he chose for his hook. Now the line sounded not only hollow to Wade, but foolish.

Glenn got out and walked into the roadhouse.

Wade looked at the glove box and thought about his dad in the bar, outnumbered by a bunch of drunken, pissed-off mill workers.

He grabbed the gun, ran out of the car, and crept up to the window, raising his head just enough to peer over the sill to see what was going on.

It looked like a tornado had swept through the place, upending tables and breaking dishes. Three big men, about as wide as the pickup trucks they drove, stood proudly in the midst of the destruction, grinning drunkenly and sweating from their exertions. Another man sat on a barstool, his back to the bar, directing the show.

A waitress cowered in the far corner, holding a rag to her bloody nose. One of her eyes was already swelling shut. A fat cook stood protectively in front of her, holding a greasy frying pan up like a shield.

As Glenn came in, the man on the stool spun around to face him. It was clear that the guy was the group leader, or at least their spokesperson, by the way the others fell in behind him.

Glenn walked up slowly to the bar and addressed the man on the stool. "You want to tell me what happened here, son?"

"We're just having a good time, that's all," said the man. "There a law against that?"

Glenn gestured to the waitress. "How did Phyllis get hurt?"

"She done that to herself," the man said.

"Clete hit me!" she said. "Twice!"

"I put her in her place," Clete said. "She ought to know better than to slap a man."

"You grabbed my ass," she said. "Nobody does that without an invitation."

"Your ass is an invitation," Clete said. "Ask anybody. Ain't that so, Deputy?"

Glenn grabbed Clete's head and slammed his face into the bar.

Wade heard Clete's nose crack like a boot stomping on dry twigs, but it may just have been his imagination filling in the blanks. It was a startling sight. He'd never seen his father hurt anyone before. But what was more surprising to Wade was how fast and naturally his father lashed out.

Like he'd done it before.

Like he was comfortable with it.

Wade shivered, but it wasn't just from the cold.

His father yanked Clete's head off the bar, letting the blood, snot, and drool drip from his face. Clete gurgled and moaned.

"I'd say you and Phyllis are even now." Glenn let go of Clete and stepped back to regard the three others. "But there's still the matter of all this damage."

One of the three men stepped forward. He was twice the width of his two buddies. He had arms like tree trunks and a chest carved in granite. At least that's how he looked to Wade.

"The only damage is gonna be to you." The huge man picked up a beer bottle by the neck and broke the end off against the edge of a table. He advanced on Glenn, holding the jagged end toward him. "We're gonna fuck you up bad for what you done to Clete."

The others picked up bottles and smashed them too, backing up their buddy as he advanced on Wade's father. Wade's heart was pounding so strong that it was almost all he could hear. His hand gripped his father's gun. He wouldn't just stand by and watch his father get beaten to death. His bladder suddenly felt like it might burst, and his whole body was shaking. He wasn't sure if it was the cold or the fear.

But for all the terror that Wade felt, his father seemed totally at ease.

Glenn didn't move or stiffen up. He just sighed and rested one hand on the top of his nightstick.

"Maybe so, but I won't go down easy. You'll be hurt. And come morning, when you're puking into your toilet and squinting through your one good eye at your teeth floating around in the vomit, you'll still have to answer for what was done here tonight. Are you ready for that?"

Glenn said it all casually, betraying not the slightest hint of anxiety or fear, as if he were discussing how the fish were biting on the lake rather than his own imminent, savage beating.

The huge man looked Glenn in the eye. Glenn looked right back at him.

The only sound in the room was Clete, making a wet gurgle as he breathed, holding his smashed nose in place with his hand, blood seeping between his fingers.

After a long moment, the huge man seemed to deflate like a punctured balloon, and so did the others, their shoulders sagging and their heads becoming too heavy for their necks.

Glenn nodded. "That's what I thought."

Wade let go of the gun and wiped his sweaty hands on his pants, his heart still thumping hard. He was astonished that he could sweat while still being so cold. The tension in his bladder was gone and he felt a new and different terror as he looked down to see if he'd wet himself. To his enormous relief, he hadn't.

"You cashed your paychecks today," Glenn said to the men. "I want to see what you've got left on the bar, right now."

The men dug into their pockets and dumped crinkled bills and loose change on the bar, some of coins clattering onto the floor.

Glenn took a quick glance at the money. "That should cover the damage, Phyllis, don't you think?"

She nodded vigorously. Wade thought she would have nodded whether it was enough money or not.

Glenn motioned to the door. "Good night, boys."

The men shuffled to the door, Clete glaring at Glenn as he staggered past him.

Wade ducked under the window and flattened himself against the side of the building as they came out, piled into their pickups, and sped off, their tires kicking up dirt and gravel as they fishtailed onto the roadway. He peered over the edge of the windowsill and looked inside again.

His father turned to Phyllis. "He was right about your ass, Phyllis. Maybe if you kept it in jeans that didn't hold it so tight, you wouldn't get in so much trouble."

Wade rushed back to the car, getting inside just as his father emerged from the roadhouse. That's when he realized that in all the excitement he'd forgotten the gun. It was on the ground under the window. But it was too late to retrieve it now.

He looked back to see his dad lean under the window, pick up the gun, and put it in his holster as if he'd left it on the ground himself.

Glenn walked back to the car and got inside. His father never said a word about it.

Wade figured that his father's advice, and the memory of that night, had saved his own life today. But this time, what Wade stood for wasn't enough. He needed his gun.

His confrontation with the Indian did more than bring back old memories. It made Wade even hungrier than he was before. As he devoured his lukewarm pancakes and bacon, Mandy stood across from him, nursing an iced tea and keeping his mug filled with hot coffee.

"Was that legal?" she asked.

"I probably should have arrested them," Wade said. "But it wasn't practical."

"I meant trashing Timo's ride," she said.

So that was the Indian's name. Wade made a mental note of it.

"It isn't a law on the books, but it's a law that everyone understands."

"An eye for an eye," she said.

"Timo can file a grievance with the department if he wants," Wade said. "He'll probably prevail and get my badge."

"That's not how he expresses his grievances or how he prevails," she said. "He's maimed people for less. I'm surprised you're sitting here instead of on your way to wherever you came from."

"I didn't finish eating," he said. "These pancakes are too good to waste."

"Aren't you worried that he'll come back?"

"I'm sure he will," Wade said, removing his napkin and rising from his stool. "I'll be back too, first thing tomorrow morning. But I've got a bunch of errands to do now, like dropping my car off at a body shop."

"You'd be a fool to come back."

"This is where I work," he said.

"Work somewhere else. This isn't someplace you want to be."

"You came back," he said.

"That's different." She glanced over at her father, who was facing a wall-mounted TV, watching one of the TV judges delivering daytime TV justice, then fixed her gaze back on Wade. "You'll die here."

"Here is as good a place as any."

Wade left a few dollars on the counter as a tip and walked out, stopping for a moment outside the door to survey the street. There was nobody waiting for him.

CHAPTER EIGHT

Wade wiped the glass off the driver's seat and drove the Mustang to a body shop that he'd seen near his hotel. With no windshield or windows, the chilly night air blew through his car like it was a convertible. He'd cranked up the heat and aimed the vents at himself, but it didn't help much.

He called his insurance company, sorted things out with them, and made it clear to the shop owner not to replace the plastic *Bullitt* crap. In fact, he asked if they could remove whatever was left of the *Bullitt* stuff inside the car as well. The shop guy thought he was nuts but agreed to do it for a few extra bucks on top of the deductible payment, since he'd have to order parts to replace the undamaged ones that they were removing. That was fine with Wade.

He rented a Ford Explorer, which was dropped off for him at the body shop, and made sure that he signed up for all the available insurance, which cost him nearly as much as renting another car. But after what had happened to his Mustang, and the likelihood of Timo's retaliation, Wade figured the insurance was a wise investment. He transferred his gun locker from the Mustang to the rear of the Explorer and drove off.

His first stop was the Home Depot, where he bought the lumber and supplies that he'd need to patch and paint the station, stain the hardwood floors in his apartment, and clean and disinfect the squad cars.

His errands finished, he grabbed a hamburger at a Jack in the Box drive-through and ate his meal in his car as he drove back to his hotel for what he knew would be his last decent night of sleep for quite a while.

————

Wade checked out of the hotel and was eating his Grand Slam breakfast at Denny's by 6:00 a.m. He was dressed in a sweatshirt and jeans because he didn't want to get his uniform dirty loading up his stuff from the storage unit.

He didn't have many belongings to move. He'd let Alison keep the house and just about everything in it because he didn't want to make things uncomfortable for her or his daughter.

That was also what had cost him his family—his desire to protect them from discomfort.

After the confrontation in Roger Malden's kitchen, and after being questioned for hours that day by the FBI and Internal Affairs, Wade returned to his New King City home to find Alison waiting for him. She was sitting at the kitchen table, watching the news on TV about the arrests. Brooke was at school.

Wade turned off the TV and sat down across from her and girded himself for another kitchen confrontation. But this time there were no guns, no terrified children. Just the two of them.

Somehow, he'd been more comfortable in Malden's kitchen a few hours earlier than he was in his own kitchen at that moment.

Alison asked him when he knew that Roger and the other officers were corrupt. He told her that he suspected it almost immediately but didn't know for sure until he'd been there about two months. That's when he decided to go to the Justice Department and begin gathering evidence.

She was silent for a time and then said, "You should have talked with me about it before you went to the Justice Department."

"What difference would it have made?"

"We could have discussed the alternatives."

He shook his head. "There were no alternatives."

"That was not for you to decide on your own," she said, her voice steadily rising until her final words were almost a shout. "We are a family."

"And that's what I was trying to protect. This wasn't about us. It was about dirty cops doing some very bad things," Wade said. "If I told you what was going on, you would have become part of it. I didn't want that."

"That's what you don't understand," she said, making a noticeable effort to keep her voice down, her anger in check. "I am a part of it. So is Brooke. What you do has consequences, and we all have to live with them."

"If I told you what was happening, you would have had to live with it every day. Every time we saw Roger, Phil, Artie, and their families you would have had to pretend not to know what I knew. They would have sensed your deception right away."

"You mean I'm not as good a liar as you are."

"I was protecting you."

"You were lying to us," she said. "Every day for two years."

"It doesn't matter now." He reached out to touch her hand but she yanked it away. "It's over."

"No, Tom, it's all just beginning. There will be a long trial, constant media attention, and a lot of ugliness."

"What other choice did I have?"

"You could have chosen us," she said.

From that night on, Wade slept in the guest room. The two of them hardly talked except when Brooke was around, but then it was only a performance for her benefit. Brooke knew it and soon became as withdrawn from them both as Alison was from him.

Late one night after the trial ended, as the glare of media attention was finally dimming, Wade sat at the kitchen table eating some leftovers. Alison came in and dropped a set of divorce papers down on the table in front of him.

He glanced at the top sheet, then up at her. "Shouldn't we talk about this?"

"Now you know how I felt," she said.

"Is that what this is, Ally? Payback?"

She shook her head. "It's consequences, Tom. You made a choice without us. You had to do what you thought was right. I'm doing the same thing."

He left the next day. All he took with him were some clothes, a few boxes of books and CDs, a TV and an entertainment center, his recliner, some photo albums, a laptop computer, a mini-fridge, and all the guest-room furniture.

He put it all into the storage unit and himself into the hotel across the street, which was another storage unit, a place to shelve himself until his life started again.

And now it finally had.

Wade had all the furniture he needed for the apartment for now. He still had to buy dishes, cutlery, and cookware, a kitchen table, and a couch, but he was in no hurry. Paper plates, plastic silverware, and fast food would do fine for the time being.

He hired some day laborers who were milling around outside the storage facility with their own truck. They loaded his stuff in less than an hour and then followed him to his new home.

As he drove, Wade kept his eye on the rearview mirror, worried that his movers would turn around when they realized where he was heading, but they stuck with him. They unloaded his belongings into the upstairs apartment with amazing speed, eager to get their money and flee.

He couldn't blame them.

While they unloaded his stuff, he taped some newspapers to the window to give himself some privacy until he could hang some drapes.

The movers dropped his box spring and mattress in the center of the living room and dumped most of his stuff around the bed. Wade hadn't given any thought to interior design yet, anyway.

He walked them back to their truck and paid them off. As the truck drove away, he noticed that his move in had attracted a crowd across the street. They all seemed stunned by the sight. An alien invasion would have drawn fewer people and less incredulity.

A couple of the guys who'd trashed his car were among the lookie-loos, but Timo wasn't one of them. His bashed-up Escalade was long gone, of course. It was a symbol of a humiliating defeat that Timo's crew couldn't let stand for all to see.

Guthrie stood outside his restaurant, leaning on his oxygen tank and smoking a cigarette. His daughter, Mandy, walked over to Wade just as the movers sped off. She was carrying a Styrofoam takeout box and a brown paper bag.

"I've seen a lot of people move out of this neighborhood," Mandy said to Wade. "But I've never seen anybody foolish enough to move in."

"I was won over by the warm welcome that I got yesterday," Wade said.

"You're crazier than I thought," she said. "Are you moving into that upstairs apartment?"

"Yeah," he said.

"The last person who lived there died, you know."

"Of old age?" he asked.

"Lead poisoning," she replied.

"From the paint?"

"From the bullets," she said. "You really must have a death wish."

"The wish isn't mine," he said.

"You're just doing your best to grant it for somebody else," she said and handed him the box and the bag. "I wish you wouldn't."

"I like your wish better," he said.

"Then you're going to pack up and get out?"

"I'm going be extra cautious and vigilant," he said, then hefted the box. "What's this?"

"Fry bread dusted with sugar, some maple syrup, and a cup of coffee. A housewarming gift. Or my contribution to your wake. I guess it depends on how the day goes."

"Thanks," he said. "I might stop by for dinner, if I'm still around by then."

"You do that. Be sure to look both ways before crossing the street," she said and turned back to her restaurant. He watched her walk away and remembered the advice that his dad had given to the waitress at the roadhouse. His father probably would have given the same advice to Mandy.

He went back inside, took a quick sip of coffee, and tore off a piece of the hot fry bread to eat on his way upstairs to change into his police uniform.

The deep-fried dough, the size of a dinner plate, was sweet and delicious and instantly addictive. If he didn't want to become morbidly obese, he'd have to start doing his patrols on foot.

Wade was back downstairs within a few minutes, and at the front counter working on the rest of the fry bread, when a blue 1968 Chevy Impala convertible pulled up to the curb. The white soft top was torn, the paint was oxidized, and rust was eating away at some of the grill.

Officer Billy Hagen emerged in uniform, a smile on his face that only got bigger once he came through the door and looked around his new station. There was a freckle-faced boyishness and natural exuberance to him that made it hard for Wade to imagine Billy projecting much authority on the street.

Billy offered his hand to Wade. "Officer Billy Hagen, sir, reporting for duty."

They shook hands. Billy had a firm grip and pumped his arm enthusiastically.

"Sergeant Tom Wade. Welcome aboard."

"Damn glad to be here, sir."

"Really?"

"This is not at all what I was expecting," Billy said.

"What were you expecting?"

"After what I heard about you, I figured you'd be some moralistic, by-the-book, hard-ass shit kicker."

"What makes you think that I'm not?"

Billy gestured to the walls. "We've got the same taste in decorating and movies, though I prefer *Asscrack Bandits 3* way more than *Asscrack Bandits 4*."

Wade had forgotten all about the porno posters. "Those posters aren't mine. They were left over from the adult DVD store that used to be here."

"Did they leave any DVDs behind?"

"I don't think so," Wade said.

"Did you look?"

"No," Wade said.

"So there's still hope," Billy said.

"You mentioned that you'd heard about me."

"They've got your face on one of the targets in the academy shooting range, mixed in with the civilians, cops, and perps," Billy said. "You counted as a perp."

"Do you have an opinion about what I did?"

Billy gestured to the fry bread. "Can I have a bite?"

"Help yourself," Wade said.

Billy tore a piece of the bread off and popped it into his mouth. "It's not my problem."

"You're a cop, aren't you?"

"Out there." Billy tipped his head to street. "Not in here."

"So it's a matter of loyalty to you."

"It's common sense." Billy took another piece of fry bread. "Even a dog doesn't shit where it sleeps."

"I see," Wade said.

"No offense meant," Billy said with a grin.

"None taken." Wade took another piece of fry bread before Billy ate it all. "Do you mind if I ask why you became a cop?"

"I didn't want to spend my life in retail, which is where I knew I was heading," Billy said. "I thought being a cop would be more exciting. You're on the move, you never know what's going to happen, and the pay is pretty good."

"What about enforcing the law? Protecting and serving your community? How do you feel about that?"

"It's my job. It isn't my religion."

Wade studied Billy, trying to figure out if his good-natured boyishness was real or a persona he adopted either to get away with things or to get people to underestimate him.

"Is this one of those Indian doughnuts?" Billy asked, licking his fingers.

"It's called fry bread," Wade said.

"Think where the tribes would be today if only they'd learned a couple hundred years ago to make 'em smaller and stick a hole in the center," Billy said. "Every Winchell's, Krispy Kreme, and Dunkin's on earth would belong to them. They'd be huge."

A Toyota Camry pulled up to the curb outside. The car was an older model, but it looked like it had just rolled off the assembly line that morning.

Officer Charlotte Greene got out of the car, an angry scowl on her face. She wore a perfectly pressed uniform, the Kevlar vest underneath it smoothing away whatever natural curves she had, but her striking beauty couldn't be blunted. Her eyes had a natural intensity that demanded attention, and once she had it, it was hard to look away from her face. She had sharply defined features that implied both strength and grace.

She marched into the station, clearly pissed off even before she came through the door. But once she did, her severe gaze shifted from Wade and Billy and immediately locked on the posters.

Charlotte put her hands on her hips and looked indignantly at the two of them as if they were children.

"This is sexual harassment, and if you think I'm going to take it simply because I'm a rookie, you're mistaken," Charlotte said. "It's bad enough that I was sent here in the first place."

"The posters were left by the previous tenant and I didn't get around to removing them." Wade said. "Things have been kind of hectic around here. I apologize for offending you."

He went over and ripped one of the posters from the wall. But he wasn't actually sorry. The reactions that the two officers had to the posters were revealing.

"Whoa," Billy said, rushing over and taking the torn poster from him. "Let me do that, Sarge. Those are works of art."

Wade turned back to Charlotte. "I'm Sergeant Tom Wade. This is Officer Billy Hagen. Welcome to—"

"Darwin Gardens," she interrupted. "I know who you are and why you're here. That doesn't explain what *I'm* doing here."

"You were in the top of your class at the police academy," Wade said.

"I'm also an African-American woman."

"I noticed," Wade said.

"I think that's what this is about," she said.

"I agree," he said.

"You do?"

"And they rewarded you for your exemplary performance by sending you to the worst neighborhood in King City."

"Exactly," she said, warming up to him. "They are marginalizing me, slapping me down because of my gender and my race."

"Where did you expect them to assign you?" Wade asked.

"Meston Heights," Charlotte said.

"But there is no crime in Meston Heights. It's one of the richest, cleanest neighborhoods in the city."

"It's where every cop wants to be," she said, narrowing her eyes at him. She knew he was playing her now. "They have the best resources of any station in the department."

"The private security officers up there outnumber the police four to one. You would have nothing to do. Is that really what you trained so hard for?"

"OK, fine," she said. "What about Central Division?"

"The only reason you'd want to work out of headquarters as a patrol officer is for the opportunity to kiss up to the brass. But that's not going to happen. They only see patrol officers as the household help. The plum assignment around there is getting to drive the chief around. Is that a job you really want? Would that make you feel good about your gender and your race?"

"You're mocking me," she said.

"I'm telling you that this is where you'll make the most impact, where you are the most needed, and where you can put both your sociology degree and your police training to use."

"We both know that isn't why I was sent here," she said. "Or why you were."

Wade shrugged. "Does the *why* really matter? You aren't going to make a difference in Meston Heights or driving the chief to Rotary Club lunches. But here you might."

"Is that what you tell yourself?"

"I started as a patrol officer in Crown Park. Robbery stats were way up, so the department offered cops a chance to work four overtime hours at the top of their shift to increase the police presence on the streets. All we were supposed to do was drive up and down the streets in our patrol cars as a high-visibility deterrent."

"I don't see what any of that has to do with me," Charlotte said.

"I had a better idea," Wade continued. "Me and my partner ditched our cars and got out on foot. We wore baseball caps and long hoodies over our uniform shirts and gun belts. We blended right into the environment, like we were invisible. Crimes went down right in front of us. We made arrests, every day, before our shifts—drug dealers, parolees on weapons violations, at-large suspects wanted in connection with open burglary, rape, and murder investigations."

"Cool," Billy said from across the room, carefully taking down one of the posters. "When do I get to do that?"

Wade ignored him. "We brought in a lot of crooks, more than we did once our official shifts started. We got noticed and moved up fast. You think that would have happened at Meston Heights?"

"You ended up in the MCU," she said. "What happened to your partner?"

"He's a homicide detective."

"How's he doing?" she asked.

Wade shrugged. He hadn't spoken to Harry Shrake since the MCU scandal broke. Harry was even angrier at Wade for not confiding in him than Alison was.

"Excuse me, Sarge." Billy stepped up to them and held the rolled-up porn-movie posters under his arm. "Can I have these? I need something to hang in my living room."

"They're all yours," Wade said.

"I guess you don't expect to bring a lot of women home," Charlotte said to Billy.

"I don't see why not," Billy said.

"They'll take one look at your artwork and walk out the door," she said.

"I didn't get your name," Billy said.

"Charlotte Greene."

"Well, Charlie, I've never had one walk out yet," Billy said. "At least not without a big smile on her face."

CHAPTER NINE

Wade showed his officers around the station, went over their duties and responsibilities, then spread out a map of downtown King City on a desk, marked off the boundaries of their patrol zone with a red highlighter, and tacked it on the wall.

"This is our beat," he said. "Our borders are Washington Boulevard to the north, the docks to the east, the projects to the south, and the freeway on the west."

It wasn't called the south side on the map anymore because, after years of decay and violence, the name carried negative connotations. Nobody wanted to be associated with the south side, least of all the city councilmen who represented the district. So the city council simply erased the name and didn't give it a new one. They said they were doing it to remove the stigma from the neighborhood, stimulate investment, and renew civic pride.

But those three things never happened, not that anybody ever expected them to. There was another reason for what they did. A place without a name doesn't exist. And neither do the people in it.

Erasing the south side in name made it a lot easier for the police to erase the rapes, murders, and robberies that occurred there from their overall crime statistics too. Crime can't exist in a place that isn't there.

The chamber of commerce certainly wasn't going to complain about it. Or the taxpayers in places like Meston Heights. With the south side factored out, crime was down in King City.

But Wade didn't share his opinions with his officers. He covered only the facts they needed to know. The rest they'd learn from experience.

Charlotte took notes in her leather-bound notebook as Wade spoke.

Billy seemed bored and antsy, tapping his foot nervously throughout the brief orientation.

"How many other officers are going to be working out of this station?" she asked Wade.

"You're looking at everybody," Wade said.

"Just the three of us?"

Wade nodded. Charlotte shot a meaningful look at Billy, who didn't seem to understand the meaning.

"What's the problem?" Billy asked her.

"It's going to be one officer to a car," she said, obviously irritated with him. "We're going to be on our own out there."

"Works for me, Charlie," he said, stifling a yawn. "I'm tired of having a babysitter. I'm ready."

Charlotte dismissed Billy with a frown and turned to Wade. "How quickly can backup get here if we need it?"

He didn't want to tell her that backup wouldn't come until it was way too late, if it ever came at all.

"Not quickly enough," Wade said. "So we're going have to act as if the entire department is just the three of us, which is why I've adjusted the traditional shift schedule."

He explained that he was creating two twelve-hour shifts, 8:00 a.m. to 8:00 p.m. and 8:00 p.m. to 8:00 a.m. The officers could flip a coin to decide who got days or nights to start off with. Then they could switch shifts each month. He'd work a 9:00 p.m. to 9:00 a.m. shift so that he could ride with them during the most dangerous hours of their shifts, but he'd remain on call at all times during his off-duty hours as their backup.

"Are we going to get paid for the overtime?" Billy asked.

"I wouldn't count on it," Wade said.

"That's against union rules," Charlotte said.

"I know. But I also know the department won't approve these shifts or authorize the overtime. They'd rather each of us went out there with only God and the dispatcher for company."

"That sounds good to me," Billy said.

"It sounds like suicide," Charlotte said, then turned to Wade. "Your plan doesn't sound much better. If I've got to call for backup while you're off duty, how are you going to get to me fast enough to save my ass?"

Wade pointed to the ceiling. "I live upstairs."

Both officers stared at him.

"You're kidding me," Charlotte said.

He shook his head. "I moved in this morning. I'll keep the radio with me at all times."

"You are hard-core," Billy said. "But not in an *Asscrack Bandits* way. More like *Walker, Texas Ranger.*"

"You're willing to live here just for us?" Charlotte asked.

"Who says it's for you?" Wade asked.

"I don't see any days off in your schedule," Billy said.

"Because there aren't any," Wade said.

"How long are we going to work like that?" Billy asked.

"Until I feel you're ready to handle a shift on your own or we get some additional manpower."

"When are you expecting those new guys to arrive?"

"I'm not," Wade said.

Charlotte mulled it over for a long moment, then surrendered with a sigh. "Fine. I'll take nights to start, if that's OK with you, Billy."

"OK by me," Billy said.

"Your first shift is tonight," Wade said. "That's it for me. Any questions?"

"You aren't wearing Kevlar, are you?" Billy asked, knocking on his own underneath his shirt as if it were a suit of armor.

"Nope," Wade said.

"Why not?" Billy asked.

"Because they're itchy and make you sweat," Charlotte said, unconsciously scratching at hers. "Especially if you're wearing a bra."

"Don't wear a bra," Billy said. "We won't mind."

"It's not about the discomfort," Wade said. "It's a personal choice. I believe that the vest tells people that you're weak, that you're afraid to get hurt."

"So does a gun," Charlotte said.

Wade shook his head. "That's different. A gun tells people that you're prepared to do whatever is necessary to enforce the law and maintain the peace."

"So does a vest," Charlotte said.

Wade shook his head again. "It undercuts you before you even walk into a situation. All you need is a badge."

"A badge doesn't cover your body," Billy said.

"It represents something," Wade said.

"But it's not bulletproof. You may not have noticed, Sarge, but there are ten-year-olds out there carrying more firepower than us. You can empty your gun into this"—Billy knocked on his chest again—"and I'll sit right up and blow your head off."

"That's the other problem with the vest," Wade said. "It gives you a sense of invincibility that you don't have. It makes you stupid."

"You're calling me stupid?" Billy asked with a cocky swagger. "With all due respect, sir, I'm not the one who thinks a badge is going to protect him."

Wade drew his gun and shot Billy in the chest.

Billy was blown off his feet and onto the floor, where he lay flat on his back, wide-eyed and gasping for breath, the wind kicked out of his lungs by the impact of the bullet.

Charlotte rushed to Billy's side. Wade holstered his gun and turned to see someone standing in the front doorway.

"May I help you?" Wade asked.

The man wore a burgundy silk tracksuit with gray trim and looked to Wade to be in his forties. He was short, tanning-parlor tan, his hair an unnatural shade of brown. But his most distinctive feature was his mangled nose, which had been broken so many times that it looked like a glob of clay. There was a gold chain around his neck, a Rolex around his wrist, and a couple of fat diamond-studded gold rings on his fingers.

"I'm Duke Fallon." The man sounded like his sinuses were filled with concrete. "And I'd like to buy you a cup of coffee."

Wade knew who Fallon was. After a bloody coup a few years earlier, Fallon became the leading crime lord in Darwin Gardens and used it as his base to expand his operations into other areas of the city. The MCU taxed Fallon on his additional revenue.

The mention of Fallon's name momentarily distracted Charlotte from Billy. She'd opened Billy's shirt to reveal a bullet caught in the Kevlar mesh in the center of the vest. There was no blood, and Billy was beginning to suck some air into his lungs again.

Wade looked past Fallon out on the street, where he could see an S-Class Mercedes parked in front of Pancake Galaxy, Timo and two of the guys he'd faced down yesterday glowering at him. There were a few people standing on the sidewalk, brought out of the shadows by either Fallon's arrival or the gunshot or maybe both.

"That'd be nice," Wade said and glanced over at Charlotte, who glared furiously at Wade. "Just give me a moment."

"Sure thing," Fallon said and stepped outside.

"The squad cars out back need to be cleaned and disinfected," Wade said to Charlotte. "I'll be across the street having coffee."

"With a man responsible for countless killings and a good chunk of the drug trade in this city."

"I'd rather meet him over a cup of coffee than the end of a gun." He shifted his gaze to Billy. "Come get me when you're ready to return fire."

Wade went outside and joined Fallon on the corner. They both took a moment to gaze out at the onlookers.

"They seem surprised to see me," Wade said.

"You can't blame them. They saw me go in and heard a gunshot," Fallon said. "They probably thought that I'd killed you."

"Why would they think that?"

"I'm told that I have a nasty temper." Fallon gestured to the station. "Apparently, you do too."

Wade looked back and saw Charlotte helping Billy to his feet. "That wasn't anger. That was a demonstration."

Fallon smiled. "I like that. A demonstration. I might steal that from you."

The two men strode diagonally across the empty intersection toward the restaurant. They took their time, everyone watching them.

"I saw you testify on TV," Fallon said. "It was like the OJ trial, only with cops instead."

The way Wade remembered it, the cops were on trial in the OJ case too—they just weren't sitting at the defendant's table.

"As I recall," Wade said, "your name came up a few times during the trial."

Fallon waved off the remark. "Nasty rumors and innuendo. But I don't care about that. I'm just glad justice was done."

"You mean you're glad you don't have to pay off the MCU anymore. You underwrote Roger's kitchen remodel."

"Is it nice?"

"He replaced the linoleum flooring with travertine and the tile countertops with granite."

"What was he thinking putting in all that rock? It must be like eating in a fucking cave," Fallon said. "How's your kitchen? Does it need updating?"

Timo crossed his arms under his chest and amped up the intensity of his glower as Wade approached the S-Class.

Wade smiled and gave Timo a little wave as he passed. "Are you offering me a home improvement loan, Duke?"

"It would be a gift," Fallon said, opening the door to the restaurant for him. "I give them to deserving individuals. It's not very hard to be deserving."

"It would be for me," Wade said and went inside.

There were no customers inside, just the Guthries and a cook in the back, an old woman with her hair in a net. Peter Guthrie sat behind the register, snorting his oxygen, and Mandy was sitting at the counter, reading a newspaper.

Fallon went to one of the window booths. Wade took a seat across from him. Mandy approached with a coffeepot.

"What will you have, gentlemen?" she asked as she filled their mugs.

"Coffee is fine for me," Wade said.

"You have any apple pie left, sweetie?" Fallon asked.

"We always save a slice for you, Duke."

"I'd kill you if you didn't," he said with a grin, then turned to Wade. "I don't like it when people leave me the crumbs."

Wade took that comment as a clumsy allusion to Fallon's reasons for overthrowing Gordon Gansa, who was dismembered while he was still alive, his body parts scattered throughout Darwin Gardens. Rumor was that Fallon cut him up with a handsaw and made Gansa's crew watch, which effectively quashed anyone's will to attempt a coup.

Mandy went off to get the pie. Wade took a sip of his coffee.

"I heard you had a little scuffle yesterday," Fallon said.

"Nothing I couldn't handle."

"You were lucky. Did you know that the last cops who came here were gunned down?"

"A couple of rookies who were pursuing a stolen car," Wade said. "I went to their funerals."

"It was a sad, tragic day," Fallon said. "I'd hate to see it happen again."

"So would I," Wade said.

Mandy came up and set a slice of pie, with a scoop of vanilla ice cream on it, in front of Fallon.

"Enjoy," she said and turned away.

"Thanks, sweetie," Fallon said and started to devour his pie.

Wade studied Fallon and sipped his coffee.

He was aware of Mandy and her father looking at them while trying to appear as if they weren't. There were no other customers to serve and the tension created by the emptiness, and the presence of Duke Fallon, was palpable.

He was aware of Timo outside, leaning against Fallon's car, staring hard at Wade. It was a wonder the window didn't shatter from the intensity of the hatred.

It was a moment or two, and several mouthfuls of apple pie à la mode later, before Fallon spoke again.

"This can be a peaceful neighborhood if everybody follows the rules."

"I agree," Wade said.

"What you and I need to have is an understanding," Fallon said.

"That would be good," Wade said.

"So here's what you need to understand. I make the laws here," Fallon said, poking himself in the chest with his thumb. "Now that you're a resident, you're going to have to follow them just like everybody else."

"What are your laws?"

"There's only one," Fallon said, leaning over the table toward Wade and looking him in the eye. "You stay out of my fucking way, or I will lay waste to your little station and everybody in it. I'd probably get a big gift basket from the chief for doing it too."

Fallon leaned back, satisfied with himself. Wade held out a napkin to him.

"You need this. You got ice cream on yourself while you were terrifying me."

Fallon looked down at the ice cream on his chest.

"Shit!" He snatched the napkin and dabbed madly at the stain, rubbing it in even deeper, matting the silk. "This is a twenty-five-hundred-dollar tracksuit."

"Maybe you should wear a bib," Wade said.

Fallon lifted his head and glared at Wade. "Maybe you should watch your fucking mouth."

Wade took a sip of coffee and set down his mug. "Has it occurred to you, Duke, that 'laying waste' to me and the police substation might be exactly what the chief wants?"

"Isn't that what I just said?"

"It's the excuse the chief needs to invade with five hundred officers, decimate your operation, and parade you and all of your crew in chains past the media."

"There'd be a lot of cop funerals before that happened."

"Yes, but what better way is there than a war on crime to rehabilitate the department's image and push the corruption scandal out of the news? You might still get that big gift basket from him, but it will be delivered to you in your prison cell."

Fallon tossed the wadded-up napkin on the table and pushed his plate away. "Either way, you lose."

"You too," Wade said.

"At least I won't be dead."

"What makes you so sure?"

Fallon mulled that possibility for a moment. "It sounds to me like we may have a common interest."

"We might," Wade said.

"So let's compromise," Fallon said.

"What do you have in mind?"

"You can walk old ladies across the street, write a few parking tickets, scold the kiddies who swipe candy from the mini-mart, and lock up the drunks who puke on the sidewalks. But you'll stay out of everything else. If you run into something you can't avoid, you come to me and I'll handle it. That way, everybody's happy."

"I have an even simpler solution."

"I'm all ears," Fallon said.

"I'll do my job the best that I can and hope that everything works out."

"That isn't a compromise," Fallon said.

"No, it isn't." Wade slid out of the booth and stood up. "Thanks for the coffee. How was the pie?"

"It's so good I fantasize about it while I'm fucking," Fallon said.

"I'll have to try it sometime," Wade said.

"I'd make it soon, if I were you," Fallon said.

CHAPTER TEN

Wade walked out of the Pancake Galaxy without acknowledging Timo's presence and strode back to the station like he was taking a casual stroll along Riverfront Park. If they were going to gun him down now, he figured that hurrying across the street wouldn't change anything.

Charlotte was waiting for him behind the counter in the station, her hands on her hips, giving him the same indignant look that she'd had on her face when she'd first walked in.

"You need some serious psychiatric help," she said.

"How's Billy?" Wade asked.

"He's outside, cleaning the cars and grinning like a fucking idiot. He thought getting shot was awesome and he wants me to try it. He's going to have an enormous bruise that will hurt like hell once the shock wears off."

"Good," Wade said.

"You could have killed him," she said.

"He wasn't getting my point," Wade said. "It was one that he needed to understand."

"Maybe you ought to shoot me too, because the only point I got is that you're mentally unstable and extremely dangerous."

"Being a cop, and surviving a potentially deadly situation, isn't about weapons or vests," Wade said. "It's about one thing."

"Luck," she said.

"The badge," he said.

"Oh, Christ," she said. "Not again."

"You've got to have confidence in what it represents and be willing to stand for it. People sense that. Or they don't, and in that case, a vest isn't going to save you."

"That's what you wanted to say when you shot Billy?"

"No," Wade said. "I wanted to say that he's stupid."

"You *did* say that."

"He wasn't listening," Wade said and walked over to his desk, where he had the gun locker that used to be in the trunk of his Mustang on the floor.

"Is your life so simple that your badge can be the answer for everything?"

"I wish it were. But it's the one answer I can always depend on."

He lifted the locker up, set it on the counter, and opened the lid. The guns he'd gathered from Timo and his crew were in evidence bags. She looked at them.

"Where did you get all these guns?"

"I recovered them on the street outside."

"They were just lying on the ground?"

"They were after I asked the people who were pointing them at me to drop them."

"How did you do that?"

"I made a persuasive argument," Wade said, closing the lid on the locker and sliding it toward her. "You need to go home and get some rest before your shift. On your way, I want you to drop these off at the crime lab at One King Plaza for ballistic and fingerprint checks against any open cases."

"I'll drop them off," she said, picking up the locker. "But I can't promise that I'll be back tonight."

"Fair enough."

Wade walked her to the door and locked it after her. Then he went out back, where Billy was drying the exterior of one of the squad cars.

"Ready for action?" Wade asked.

"Hell yes," Billy said and tossed his rag.

——

They moved their personal vehicles into the fenced-in parking lot behind the station for safety and headed out in a squad car that smelled like piss-scented disinfectant.

Wade drove and Billy called in their status to the dispatcher, a woman who sounded startled to hear from them.

"We're officially open for business," Wade said.

"What do you think our first radio call will be?" Billy asked, playing with the hole in his shirt.

"Someone reporting the discovery of a corpse."

"That's optimistic," Billy said.

"It's the only reason anybody down here ever calls the police. And even then, it's only because they can't take the smell anymore."

"I know how they feel." Billy rolled down his window.

Wade rolled down his window too.

They headed east toward the river and cruised slowly past the derelict King Steel complex of warehouses, foundries, machine shops, and welding sheds.

The cavernous buildings were decaying. The windows were shattered, the weathered bricks were covered with graffiti, and the rusted, corrugated metal siding was peeling off like flakes of dry skin.

Between the buildings, Wade caught glimpses of the river and the pilings that poked through the water, all that remained of the jetties that had eroded away against the relentless pounding of the current.

There were a dozen abandoned factories along the shoreline. The rusted tangles of pipes, gantries, tanks, conveyor belts, and smokestacks looked to Wade like massive piles of entrails that had spilled from the guts of disemboweled iron giants.

The giants bled thousands of jobs, turning what had been a prosperous working-class neighborhood into a blighted, crime-ridden hellhole. But many of the giants survived their wounds and moved to Mexico, India, Asia, and South America.

The vast parking lots around the factories were cluttered with discarded furniture and appliances, the hulks of stripped automobiles, and dry weeds as tall as cornstalks. Scraps of snagged plastic bags and paper fluttered like flags in the razor wire that ringed the tops of the cyclone fences that surrounded the dilapidated properties.

Most of the restaurants and bars that had once lined the opposite side of the street and served the factory workers were boarded up and decaying. The few that managed to remain were in disrepair, their paint chipped and faded, their signs missing letters and lightbulbs.

The few people that Wade saw on the street matched their environment. They limped along, old and weathered, decaying and abandoned. He guessed that they were the same men and women who'd once hung out in those same bars after work, but now that the work was gone, they spent their days there too.

Only a couple of the people bothered to look up at the squad car as it cruised along, and those who did regarded the officers with weariness and disdain.

It made Wade angry. Not at the people on the streets, but at the police department for deserting this place after the mills and factories did, ceding the south side to poverty and crime because the big tax dollars just weren't there anymore.

Wade faced huge obstacles establishing a beachhead against crime in Darwin Gardens, but he knew that his biggest battle wouldn't be making the streets safer—it would be proving to anyone who lived there that the police gave a damn, that they could be relied upon, and that they were worthy of respect.

It would be hard to prove because they were lies.

The department *didn't* care. They would abandon this place again the instant Wade and his rookies were taken down.

The people didn't know that, of course. They knew the new station wasn't opened to serve their interests, though, but for some other, political purpose. They knew that the patrols wouldn't last, that it was just part of the show.

They knew all that to be true because they no longer existed, a fact underscored whenever they looked at a King City map, or at their desolate streets, or at their own sorrowful reflections in the mirror.

He turned the corner and headed east on Clements Street, working his way into the former Belle Shore housing tract that was built for the factory workers in a postwar wave of prosperity and optimism.

The homes were one-story, identical stucco boxes, built fast and cheap with detached garages that opened onto rear alleys. Over the years, some homeowners had tried to spruce up and individualize their houses by adding siding, brick, or stone, window planters or exterior shutters, and by building new rooms. The clumsy results reminded Wade of the shoeboxes his daughter's preschool class had decorated with ribbons, glitter, macaroni noodles, buttons, and globs of Elmer's glue.

As he drove down the street, Wade decided that the real money to be made in Darwin Gardens wasn't from drugs, prostitution, gambling, or other crimes. It was in wrought iron. Every home had bars on the windows, iron-mesh screens on the doors, and wrought iron fences around the property.

There were no white picket fences here.

Most of the residents had let their plants die, using their fenced-in front yards as dumps, storage areas, dog runs, or parking lots for their motorcycles, boats, and cars.

The vehicles were almost always newer, more upscale, and much better maintained than the houses they were parked in front of.

It made no sense to Wade.

To him, cars were simply machines to get you from one place to another, but a home was something more than shelter. It was where you *lived*. He couldn't understand how anyone could value a car more than a nice home.

The few houses that were well kept stood out dramatically from the rest, their fresh paint, blooming flowers, and green lawns giving them a surreal, Technicolor glow, like Munchkinland in *The Wizard of Oz*.

There were more people out on the streets here than Wade had seen so far in the rest of Darwin Gardens. They sat on couches on their front porches, hung up laundry on the line, and worked on their cars. Children played in their yards while teenagers huddled on the sidewalks in groups, their smiles turning to sullen glowers as the squad car passed.

Wade turned into one of the alleys, which was strewn with trash, broken grocery carts, soiled mattresses, stripped cars, rusted pipes, and cardboard boxes. The sides of the alley were lined with cyclone or wrought iron fences and graffiti-covered cinder block walls topped with razor wire. It made the backyards of the homes resemble prison yards.

Except for one yard, where a lush garden flourished behind the wrought iron fence. The centerpiece of the garden was a burbling fountain that spilled down a stack of rocks into a tiny pond that was surrounded by colorful flowers.

There was a man in filthy clothes standing on a crate outside the fence and pissing through the bars into the pond.

"Son of a bitch," Wade said.

He gave a short burst of the siren, the loud noise startling the man so much that he tumbled off the crate, pissing into the air as he fell.

Billy laughed. "I wish I had that on tape."

Wade got out and marched over to the man, who was scrambling to stuff himself back into his pants and zip up his fly. The man was in his thirties, with an enormous head of matted hair that looked like the end of a dirty mop. The skin on his arms was covered with dry scabs and fresh sores.

"What the hell did you do that for?" the man asked, sitting up. His gums had receded so far Wade could almost see the roots of his teeth. The man was obviously a crack addict.

"You were pissing on that nice garden," Wade said. He glanced over his shoulder and was pleased to see Billy standing behind his open passenger door, backing him up as if they were handling a traffic stop.

"There's no law against pissing," the man said.

"Actually, there is," Wade said. "Urinating in public is illegal. So is indecent exposure and vandalism."

"I was just pissing," the man said. "There was no place else to go."

"You had the whole alley to piss on, but you dragged over a crate, stood on top of it, and aimed at the fountain."

"I got to aim at something."

Someone started clapping. Wade turned to see an elderly woman in a shapeless, flowered housedress and slippers applauding as she walked across the garden to the fence. Her face was blotched with age spots and she wore glasses that magnified the size of her eyes to horrific proportions. But Wade could see the adorable, bespectacled young woman that she'd once been. That woman was still there under the wrinkles, the gray hair, and the sagging body. It was how he saw his mother, right up until the end.

"Thank you so much, Officer," she said. "You have no idea how many of my flowers he's killed."

"What's your name, ma'am?"

"Dorothy Copeland," she said.

"I'm Tom Wade, the sergeant at your local police station. The officer behind me is Billy Hagen."

"We have a police station?" she asked.

"You do now." He looked back at the man, who was in a sitting position on the ground. "What have you got against Mrs. Copeland's garden?"

"She's a crazy old bitch," the man said. "Always yelling at people."

"He makes a huge mess in the alley," she said. "Look what I swept up this morning."

She opened the lid of a garbage can. Wade glanced inside and saw syringes, beer bottles, fast-food wrappers, and used condoms on top of her neatly bagged trash.

"He left all of that?" Wade asked.

"He and his drug-addict friends come at night while I'm watching my programs," she replied. "I try so hard to keep things clean, but the mess never ends."

Wade regarded the man again. "What's your name?"

"Terrill Curtis," he said, scratching at his arm.

"You're under arrest, Mr. Curtis, for public urination and vandalism."

"You're shitting me," Terrill said.

"Stand up, put your hands on your head, and lean facedown over the hood of car," Wade said.

Terrill did as he was told. Wade read him his rights as he patted him down, discovering a switchblade, a crack pipe, and a tiny square of aluminum foil, which he unfolded to reveal a pebble of crack cocaine.

"We're charging you with possession of illegal narcotics on top of everything else," Wade said.

Terrill glared threateningly at the woman.

Wade handcuffed Terrill and spun him so they were face-to-face.

"Mrs. Copeland and her garden are under my protection, Mr. Curtis. Whatever happens to her, or her flowers, will happen to you, whether you are the one responsible for it or not."

"What if somebody else pisses on them?"

"Then I will piss on you," Wade said.

"That's not fair," he whined.

"I got to aim at something," Wade said and led Terrill over to Billy. "Put him in the car."

While Billy got Terrill into the backseat, Wade went to the trunk, opened it, and took out a bullhorn, which he carried over to Mrs. Copeland.

"I'll be back in the next day or two to check on you. In the meantime, Mrs. Copeland, I want you to have this." He gave her the bullhorn. "You see anybody making a mess in the alley, just press the red trigger and yell at them with this. If that doesn't work, you give me a call, any time of the day or night."

He wrote his number down on a piece of paper and handed it to her.

"I can't believe you're doing all this for me," she said.

"It's my job, Mrs. Copeland."

"This used to be such a nice neighborhood," she said. "You should have seen it."

"I still can." Wade motioned to her garden. "Right here."

CHAPTER ELEVEN

"It smells like piss in this car," Terrill whined from the backseat as they continued their patrol.

"Then you should feel right at home," Billy said and then looked at Wade. "Why did we bother arresting him? He's not exactly a major felon."

"He is to Mrs. Copeland," Wade said.

And he was sure that she was already talking about the arrest to all of her friends. Word would spread quickly, especially after she started using the bullhorn to yell at the junkies and hookers in the alley.

The news wouldn't irritate guys like Fallon and Timo much, but Wade hoped it might give the law-abiding residents some comfort.

"What Terrill said was true," Billy said.

"Which was what?"

"Nobody pees on the dirt. We always have to pee against a tree or a bush or a rock."

"It's instinct," Wade said.

"You think it's about marking territory."

"I think it's about aiming," Wade said.

"So we're using our dicks like guns," Billy said.

"Dicks came before guns," Wade said.

"So we're using our guns like dicks."

"Most of the time," Wade said.

The blocks that followed were a mix of small homes and boxy, two-story apartment buildings built over open carports. On the retail boulevards, the liquor stores were as ubiquitous as the Starbucks coffeehouses were in New King City. There seemed to be a liquor store on every corner, second only in number to the nail salons.

He wondered if the women here were really passionate about decorating their nails or if they just enjoyed getting high on the fumes.

He kept heading east until he reached the freeway, the massive concrete interchange looming over the warren of small warehouses, repair shops, and storage units on the street and casting them in constant shadow.

One of the warehouses had a line of street people leaning against the wall out front, waiting to get inside. "Mission Possible" was painted in big letters on the windowless white cinder block. Wade wondered what the building was before it was a mission.

There was a man in a short-sleeve black shirt with a clerical collar and blue jeans walking down the line passing out water bottles from a shoulder bag. He appeared to Wade to be in his late twenties, with a shading of a beard that looked like it had been applied with a black marker to give his chin definition.

Wade pulled up to the curb and got out, meeting the priest on the sidewalk beside the police car.

The priest looked past Wade to Terrill Curtis in the backseat. "It's a little early for you to be dropping people off here, isn't it?"

"I don't know," Wade said. "Is it?"

"At least you had the courtesy to stop your car before kicking him out."

"This isn't his destination. He's on his way to jail. I just stopped by to introduce myself and to let you know we're here if you ever need us. I'm Sergeant Tom Wade and this is Officer Billy Hagen."

Billy nodded from his seat in the car. "We're working out of the new substation across from the Pancake Galaxy."

"I'm sorry, Sergeant," the man said, offering his hand. "I'm Ted Fryer, but everyone calls me Friar Ted—you know, like Friar Tuck."

"Cute," Wade said, shaking the man's hand.

"But I'm not actually a friar, or an ordained priest," Friar Ted said.

"Then why are you wearing a collar?" Billy asked through the open window.

"To show my faith. I used to be one of them," Friar Ted said, gesturing to the row of transients. "Until I was saved two years ago."

"By Jesus," Billy said.

"By a 2003 GMC Yukon," Friar Ted said. "I was high, staggered into the street, and got run over. I broke every bone in my body. It's hard to score any crack when you're in traction."

"Bet I could do it," Terrill said.

"I was also a captive audience for the bored hospital pastor. He read aloud to me from the Bible for hours every day. It led me to God."

"It would have led me to drugs," Billy said.

Ted looked back at the line. "I tried to lead them to him, but some just can't be saved. But I know he loves them anyway."

Wade nodded toward Terrill. "Does the guy in the backseat live here? Is that why you thought we were bringing him back?"

Friar Ted glanced at Terrill. "I've seen him around. He's come inside a few times for a hot meal, but he doesn't live here. I saw the police car and a drug addict in the backseat and jumped to the wrong conclusion. I apologize."

"You must have had a good reason," Wade said.

"The only time I see the police is at night as they are speeding away."

"Away from what?" Wade asked.

"The vagrants and junkies that they've removed from another neighborhood and dumped like trash on our doorstep," Friar Ted said. "That's how I got here."

"The police dropped you off?"

"The hospital did," Friar Ted said.

Wade took a deep breath and let it out slowly. "How often does this happen?"

"Pick a night," Friar Ted said.

"I will," Wade said.

———

They took Terrill back to the station. Wade filled out the necessary paperwork while Billy photographed and fingerprinted Terrill. Billy asked the drug addict if he wanted to make a call, but he didn't, so he was placed in one of the holding cells.

"What now?" Billy asked, sitting down in a chair beside Wade's desk.

"We call the dispatcher and request that a unit pick up Terrill and transport him to jail to await arraignment."

"How long is that going to take?"

"I don't know," Wade said. "It will be interesting to find out."

"You're easily interested," Billy said.

Wade radioed the dispatcher. He spent the next few hours patching all the holes in the wall with the exception of the one left by the fire. That hole would take more than Spackle to fill, and he didn't feel like cutting lumber yet.

Billy killed the time by searching every nook and cranny in the station for forgotten porn DVDs. Much to Wade's surprise, and Billy's delight, he found one. Billy was as giddy as kid after an Easter egg hunt.

By 6:00 p.m., it was getting dark and the car for Terrill still hadn't come. Wade doubted that it ever would.

"Tell you what, Billy. Why don't you take one of the squad cars, drop off Mr. Curtis at the jail, see him through processing, and go on home."

"What about my car?"

"You can leave it here overnight," he said.

"In this neighborhood?"

"It's parked at a police station," Wade said. "How much safer could it be?"

There was only one correct answer to that question and Billy knew it. And if he didn't, Wade's glare told him so.

"Right, of course," Billy said, gathering up his DVD and posters. "We're the King City Police. What was I thinking?"

He might have put up a stronger argument if he'd known what had happened to Wade's Mustang. But he didn't. And Wade wasn't about to tell him.

"It was a good first day, Billy."

"It sure was," Billy said with a grin. "I got shot and I'm leaving with free porn. It doesn't get much better than that."

There wasn't the slightest trace of bitterness or sarcasm in the remark. When Wade looked at Billy's face, what he saw was genuine delight.

At least someone was happy to be in Darwin Gardens—or was too clueless to realize how much danger he was in.

———

Wade had two hours before his next twelve-hour shift, so he headed to Pancake Galaxy for an early dinner and plenty of caffeine.

But if he was honest with himself, and he usually was, it wasn't really the food, or the convenience, that led him across the street. He wanted to see Amanda Guthrie again.

There were about a dozen customers in the restaurant, most of them middle-aged. Mandy worked the front counter while another waitress, a good twenty years older than she, covered the tables. Old man Guthrie was at the cash register with his oxygen tank, his cigarettes, and his shotgun.

"You're still alive," Guthrie said.

"So are you," Wade said.

"The odds were more in my favor."

Wade took a seat at the counter. Mandy came over and poured him a cup of coffee.

"How was your first day?" she asked with a smile.

"You'll have to ask me tomorrow," he said. "It's not over yet."

"What are your hours?"

"Today it's twenty-four, but starting tomorrow, my shift is nine at night to nine in the morning."

"Yikes. I'll make you a canteen of coffee that you can take with you tonight."

"That would be nice," he said.

"Everybody's talking about you," Mandy said. "Your showdown with Timo, you moving in, the sit-down with Duke, your arrest of that junkie."

"Word gets around," he said.

"Isn't that what you wanted?"

It was and she got points in his book for knowing it.

"So what's the consensus?" he asked.

"Duke bought you, or you'd already be dead."

"What do you think?"

"I think if you could be bought, you'd still be in the Major Crimes Unit and not here."

"You read up on me," he said.

"I did," Mandy said. "What would you like for dinner?"

"The usual."

"You've only been here once."

"Now you know how much I liked it."

She took the order back to the cook in the kitchen and then served some other patrons at the counter.

While Mandy did that, two of the guys who'd trashed Wade's car came in and approached Guthrie. But they kept their eyes on Wade, staring at him with cold hate.

Wade just sipped his coffee, unperturbed by their presence, which perturbed them plenty.

Without a word, Guthrie opened the register, took out some money, and handed it to them. They walked out.

Wade had another sip of coffee. "Donating to charity?"

"Paying my weekly security bill," Guthrie said.

"I thought this was hallowed ground."

"Even the Vatican needs security," Guthrie said.

"I don't recall seeing any smiling pancakes on the walls of the Sistine Chapel."

"If you look closely, they're there," Guthrie said. "Michelangelo hid pancakes everywhere. It was his thing."

"Have you thought about not paying?" Wade asked.

"The DVD place tried that," Guthrie said. "They had a fire and now they're gone."

"But now you've got a police station right across the street," Wade said. "That changes things."

"We'll see," Guthrie said and starting coughing.

Mandy came out of the kitchen with Wade's pancakes and bacon and carried them to an empty booth by the window. She set the plates down on the table and came back to the counter.

"Your dinner is getting cold," she said.

He picked up his coffee and went over to the booth. A moment later, Mandy slid into the bench seat across from him, setting down the pot of coffee and half of an apple pie.

"What are we doing over here?" Wade asked as he started to eat.

"I wanted some privacy while I chatted with you."

"Do you want to tell me something that you don't want your father to overhear?"

"I might say something racy and suggestive."

"Like what?"

She picked up a fork and took a bite of his pancakes. "I haven't had sex in six months."

"Oh," Wade said.

"Aren't you going to ask me why?"

"Nope," Wade said, continuing to eat. He liked how frank she was and how relaxed she seemed to be with him. It made him feel relaxed, more at ease than he'd felt in months. The uniform did too, though he didn't know why.

"Aren't you interested?" she asked.

"Sure I am," he said. "But I'm being chivalrous."

She stole another bite of his pancakes. "I didn't know that chivalry involved not talking about sex."

"Sir Lancelot never talked about sex."

"But he got plenty of it," she said.

"Probably," Wade said.

"That's why they called it Camelot," she said.

"I think you're mispronouncing it," he said.

"What about you, Tom?"

"What about me, Mandy?"

"Are you getting plenty of it?"

"No," he said.

"Any?"

"I'm not very good at this."

"I doubt that," she said. "I think you're a man who doesn't do anything unless you're certain that you're good at it."

"What I mean is that I was married for a long time."

"But you aren't anymore," she said.

He shook his head. "I'm not sure I know how to be with someone else anymore."

"Do you want to be?"

"I didn't until now," he said.

She took another bite of his pancakes. "Maybe you should be less chivalrous."

He pushed aside his plate and she slid the pie in front of him.

"Want some apple pie? It's my momma's recipe."

"I'm told it's better than sex."

"I think we ought to do a comparison," she said. "While the taste is still fresh in our mouths."

She stuck a fork into the pie, carved out a bite, and ate it.

———

They made love with tender urgency on the bare mattress amid all of his unpacked boxes in the center of his apartment.

When it was over, she lay naked on top of him, her head on his chest.

"Was it Camelot?" he asked.

"I think you're mispronouncing it," she said.

"Just following your lead," he said.

"You followed it well," she said.

He stroked her back and sniffed her hair. He wanted to remember her smell, to always have that intimate recognition of her no matter what happened next.

"Why me?" he asked.

"You mean, why did I pick you to end my celibacy?"

"Yeah," he said.

"Because I know I can trust you. I didn't think I would be able to trust a man again," she said. "I also like the way you move, especially on top of me."

"You didn't know that before tonight."

"I had a strong inkling," she said. "Why did you accept my invitation to bed?"

"I'm a man," he said.

"You really are, maybe more than any man I've known," she said. "But not in that way. You wouldn't fuck a woman just because she asked you to."

"I might," he said. "Just to be chivalrous."

"I want a straight answer."

"You're smart and you're direct. You are who you are. You don't make excuses for it and you don't try to be anything else. I like that."

"It's what you like in yourself."

"You're also a very attractive woman. You mentioned that you've been away for a while. Where were you?"

"It wasn't prison, a mental institution, or a convent."

"That's a relief." Wade looked over her shoulder at the watch on his wrist. It was nearly 8:00 p.m. He hated to say what he had to say next. "Officer Greene will be here in a few minutes to start her shift. I need to go. I'm sorry, I wish I didn't have to."

"Me too." She kissed his chin and rolled off him onto her back. "But we'll have other opportunities."

He looked at her. "That would be nice."

"Nicer than my momma's apple pie?"

"Much," he said.

CHAPTER TWELVE

Wade let Charlotte drive the squad car to give her a chance to feel in control of her situation and to discover the neighborhood on her own. But mostly, he did it because he was feeling pleasantly, postcoitally languid and wanted to enjoy it. She kept stealing suspicious glances at him and he pretended not to notice.

"You didn't seem surprised to see me," she said.

"I shot Billy, not you. It's not bothering him any."

"Because he's an idiot."

"He's smarter now than he was yesterday," Wade said.

"I came back because I realized all that bullshit you said about this being the one place I could make a difference actually wasn't bullshit."

"Good to know. What did forensics say when you dropped off the guns?"

She gave him a long look, clearly disappointed that he wasn't treating her admission with the gravity she felt it deserved. He looked out the window at the dark, abandoned factories.

"They asked if it was related to a specific case."

"What did you tell them?"

"I told them that the weapons were recovered on the street outside of our station," she said.

"Did they give you an idea when we might get the fingerprint and ballistic results on the guns?"

"I got the impression it would be after hell froze over," she said. "But before dogs have evolved to the point where they can walk upright and speak English."

His cell phone vibrated on his gun belt. He'd forgotten that it was there and that it was on.

"Excuse me," he said and answered the call. "Wade."

"It's me, Dad," Brooke said.

The instant he heard her voice he felt a deep, painful stab of guilt. It must have shown on his face, because Charlotte immediately looked away and concentrated intensely on her driving.

"Where have you been?" Brooke continued.

"I am so sorry," Wade said. "I've been totally distracted by work."

"You're working?" She sounded like a young, innocent version of Ally. They shared the same vocal patterns, even the same laugh.

"Yeah," he said.

"What are you doing?"

"What I've always done. I'm a cop."

"I thought you weren't anymore," she said.

"I never stopped being one," he said. "But now I'm back on the job."

"Mom said that would never happen."

"I guess she was mistaken," Wade said.

"Will I still see you this weekend?"

"Every weekend," Wade said. "I'll come by on Saturday morning and take you to the movies. But it will have to be an early show. I'm working nights."

But even in daylight, he would still hesitate to leave Charlie and Billy alone even for a few hours. He'd take her to one of the downtown multiplexes so he wouldn't be too far from the station if his rookies got into trouble.

"What do you want to see?" Brooke asked.

"Anything that doesn't have cartoon animals."

"I'm thirteen, Dad. I am way past that. It's Mom who isn't."

Ally wasn't past a lot of things, Wade thought.

"See you Saturday," he said. "Sweet dreams."

"You too, Dad." She kissed the receiver and hung up.

Wade stuck the phone back on his belt and saw Charlotte steal a glance at him. "That was my daughter. She's thirteen."

"How many kids do you have?"

"Just the one," he said.

"How long were you married?"

"Fourteen years," he said.

"What happened?"

"I went to the Justice Department and told them that everyone I was working with in the Major Crimes Unit was corrupt."

"So your wife felt that you were betraying the department."

"She didn't know about any of it until it was over."

Charlotte turned to look at him, dismayed. "You didn't tell her?"

"It seemed like the right thing to do at the time."

Charlotte shook her head and kept driving, heading south. She slowed as they passed Duke Fallon's strip club, a windowless place called Headlights that was known for the giant neon sign shaped like a woman, her boobs flashing. It was just one of Fallon's legitimate businesses in King City and his headquarters in Darwin Gardens. Wade wondered if the choice was influenced by *The Sopranos* or if Fallon just liked being around topless women. Maybe it was both.

They kept heading south until they reached the projects, the southernmost boundary of Darwin Gardens, where the river curved in a wide arc toward the east. Wade was sure they weren't there by accident. Charlotte was smart and had probably spent the hours since he'd last seen her researching the neighborhood instead of getting rest.

The three twenty-story apartment towers were enormous tombstones marking the death of King City's industrial core. The Alphabet Towers, named after the A, B, and C buildings that comprised the triangular complex, were built in the late 1970s as premium residences for the well-paid white-collar workers who wanted to be close to their executive offices at the south side factories.

But in the last twenty years, with the fall of the factories, the towers had gone from swanky to skanky, teeming with poverty-stricken families living in slum-like conditions. Now they were known collectively as the Projects.

They were high-rise slums, except for the penthouses, which were owned by Duke Fallon. He'd restored the building B penthouse that he lived in far beyond its previous grandeur, complete with an outdoor pool, a driving range, and an unrestricted, 360-degree view of the entire city.

Fallon's penthouses in the other towers supposedly housed his most sensitive criminal enterprises, including the labs where he produced meth and processed heroin and cocaine for sale on the street.

Wade could appreciate Fallon's choice for his home base. The towers were easy to defend from attack, from the ground or the air, whether it came from gangland rivals or law enforcement. There were surveillance cameras everywhere and lookouts posted on the rooftops. And the twenty floors of slum apartments overflowing with poor families loyal to Fallon offered the crime lord plenty of human shields, creating a potential for devastating collateral damage that kept the King City police, the DEA, and the FBI from attempting raids.

At street level, the property was ringed with a wrought iron fence, surveillance cameras, and steely eyed men dressed in black who patrolled the perimeter. The men were undoubtedly armed from their black boots to their black berets.

Wade shared all of this information with Charlotte as they drove past the towers, but he had the feeling she knew it all already and was just playing along.

"Do you think we can take him down?" she asked.

"Not tonight," Wade said.

———

Wade and Charlotte stopped in at a few liquor stores and mini-marts to introduce themselves to the clerks, the people they were most likely to meet again as robbery victims. None of the clerks seemed particularly happy to meet them.

Even so, Wade bought snacks or soft drinks for the station in each store they visited, just to be sociable.

He'd taken over the driving at some point and parked them in the shadows on a side street with a view of Mission Possible.

"What are we doing here?" she asked.

"Eating," he said, tearing open a bag of Cheetos and offering her the first handful.

She declined. They sat there in silence for another forty-five minutes, watching hookers and drug dealers ply their trade, much to Charlotte's obvious, and increasing, discomfort.

"Something bothering you?" Wade asked, washing down his dinner of Cheetos and CornNuts with a Coke.

"We're seeing flagrant drug use, public drunkenness, and prostitution."

"It appears so."

"But we aren't doing anything about it."

"Nope."

"Even though we are officers of the law and these are illegal activities that we are witnessing."

"Yep."

"So why aren't we arresting anybody? Or at least giving a few stern warnings?"

"There isn't much a person down here can do to escape their troubles besides getting high or having sex, and I'd feel bad punishing them for it."

"You're joking," she said.

"We have to pick our battles."

"In other words, we're going to arbitrarily decide which laws are worth enforcing and which aren't."

"I wouldn't put it like that," he said.

"How would you put it?"

"There's only three of us, and we can't possibly take on all of the crime that's happening here. There's just too much of it. We are outnumbered and outgunned."

"Then what are we doing here?"

"The same thing we are doing everywhere else."

"You've lost me," she said.

"The police are always outnumbered and outgunned, Charlotte. The difference is that everywhere else, the people respect the law, abide by it, and expect the police to enforce it. Here, they don't. That's what we've got to change. We have to convince the community that the law matters and that it will make their lives better."

Charlotte gave him a skeptical look. "And you think we can do that by buying junk food from liquor stores and letting the hookers, drug dealers, and drunks do as they please?"

If he'd been talking to a superior officer, he would have characterized his strategy as fluid, offering maximum flexibility to react to the ever-changing situation in the field with an appropriate and measured response. But since he was talking to a rookie police officer, this is what he said:

"Yeah, that sounds about right."

A sheriff's squad car rolled through the intersection in front of them and stopped at the curb outside of the mission. Wade started the car.

Charlotte noticed. "What's up?"

Wade didn't answer. He watched as a deputy shaped like a pear got out of the passenger side of car, opened the back door, and dragged a woman out of the backseat.

The woman had matted hair and a weather-beaten face and wore five or six layers of filthy clothes. The deputy dumped her on the sidewalk and hiked up his pants in a futile attempt to keep them from riding under his gut.

Wade hit the gas and peeled out of the side street, startling the deputy and coming to a screeching halt in front of the squad car.

Before Charlotte could ask what was happening, Wade had already bolted out of the cruiser and was marching toward the second deputy, who'd practically leapt out of the driver's seat of his car onto the street.

"What do you boys think you're doing?" Wade asked, walking right past the second deputy as if he weren't even there, to confront the one who'd yanked the woman out of the car.

"Bringing this woman back home," Deputy Pear said.

"I see." Wade crouched beside the filthy woman. "Where do you live, ma'am?"

The woman was missing a good many teeth, and the ones she had left didn't look as if they'd be staying much longer. Her gums had receded nearly to the bone.

"Under the overpass by Lincoln Park," she said.

Wade looked up at the deputy. "Lincoln Park is out in Tennyson."

By this time, both Charlotte and the second deputy were standing a few feet behind Wade. It was the second deputy who spoke up.

"And if you've been out there, you know it's a nice area, real clean, full of families and kids. She belongs here."

This deputy was more muscled than his partner and had a crew cut that was so short it wasn't clear why he bothered to keep any hair at all.

Wade stood up and looked over at Charlotte to see how this was playing with her. She had her hands on her hips and a glare on her face that was even more judgmental than the one she'd given him after he'd shot Billy. He liked that.

"You can't take people off your streets and drop them here," Wade said.

"It's no different than taking the trash to the dump," Deputy Crew Cut said.

Charlotte spoke up, her body rigid with anger. "It's kidnapping."

"Call it what you like, but that's how things are done, and there's nothing you can do about it," Crew Cut said, then shared a glance with his partner. "Let's go, Fred."

The two deputies started back to their car. Wade thought about what Charlotte had just said and came to a quick decision.

"You're not going anywhere," Wade said. "You're both under arrest."

The deputies stopped, but only so they could turn around and laugh at the two cops.

"Fuck yourself," Deputy Pear said.

Wade drew his gun and shot out the rear tires of the squad car with two quick shots. The deputies instinctively went for their guns, but Charlotte had already drawn hers, though she seemed surprised to see it in her hand.

"You're crazy," Deputy Crew Cut said to Wade.

"So there's no telling what I might do next," Wade said. "If I were you, I'd play it safe, drop your guns, Tasers, batons, and pepper spray, and assume the position on your vehicle."

They glanced over to Charlotte, to see if she was wavering in her resolve, but she was standing her ground.

"You heard the man," she said.

The deputies did as we they were told but were mightily pissed off about it.

The gunshots had drawn out Friar Ted and everyone else in Mission Possible, who stared in stunned disbelief as Charlotte cuffed each of the deputies, read them their rights, and led them to the police car.

Wade gathered the deputies' weapons, put them in the trunk of his car, then helped the homeless woman to her feet and set her in the backseat with them for the ride back to the station, which they made in silence.

CHAPTER THIRTEEN:

Once they got to the station, Charlotte led the two deputies to the holding cell, uncuffed them, and locked them inside. Wade took the woman to a seat at Billy's desk and gave her a bottled water. Charlotte gestured to Wade and met him at the counter.

"You won't arrest prostitutes and drug dealers, but you'll arrest two sheriff's deputies," she said, her voice low so the others wouldn't hear them.

"I'm picking my battles," Wade said.

"You're starting wars."

"Do you disapprove of what I've done?"

She glanced back at the deputies in the cell, who were both making calls on their cell phones. "Actually, much to my astonishment, I don't."

"I'm glad to hear you say that." Wade reached into his pocket and handed her a crumpled twenty-dollar bill. "Do me a favor and get this lady something hot to eat and make her comfortable. I'm going to try to get a few hours' sleep before morning."

She tipped her head toward the cells. "What about the paperwork on them?"

"Start filling it out," he said.

"I'm going to tell it the way it happened," she said.

"I would expect nothing less," he said. "Get me if anything comes up."

Wade made the long commute up the two flights of stairs to his new home. He undressed, plugged his phone into the charger on top of one of the boxes, and went to take a shower. He let the shower run for five minutes, waiting for the muddy-brown tinge to clear and for the water to heat up. It must have been years since anybody had used the shower. The water was lukewarm when he got in, but it felt good anyway after his long day. It washed away the tension.

A lot had happened since the previous morning, but what stuck with him most was the intimate relationship that had developed with Mandy. It was a change in his life he hadn't seen coming, and now that it was here, he wasn't quite sure how to handle it.

Then again, that was becoming a familiar feeling in his life lately. Ever since his first meeting with the Justice Department, every day felt like he was venturing into unexplored territory. Some people craved that discomfort, that mystery. It made their lives exciting. He preferred predictability and routine. Excitement wasn't something he valued much.

He decided to deal with Mandy the same way he tackled everything else—he'd take things as they came and trust his instincts, not that they'd served him too well lately. That same approach had landed him in Darwin Gardens, living alone in a squalid apartment, the last fourteen years of his life packed in a dozen cardboard boxes.

And yet, he felt more centered, and more sure of himself, than he had in years.

Wade dried off, wrapped a towel around his waist, and went into the living room, where he unpacked some sheets and blankets from a box and tossed them on the mattress in a clump.

He tossed the towel, slipped on a pair of boxers, and crawled onto the mattress, pulled the mass of sheets and blankets over himself, and went to sleep.

———

It seemed like only seconds later when he was awakened by his ringing phone, but the sunlight coming through the newspapers taped to his windows told him at least a few hours had passed. He grabbed the cell phone from the charger and answered the call, his teeth sticky and tongue dry.

"Yeah," he said.

"Sorry to wake you, Sergeant," Charlotte said. He could tell from the stiff and formal tone in her voice that she was not alone. "There's an assistant district attorney here who'd like to speak with you."

"I'll be right down," Wade said.

He pulled on a T-shirt and a pair of sweats, washed his mouth out with Listerine, spit it out in his kitchen sink, and then trudged barefoot down the stairs to the station.

Because he was groggy, and still not entirely used to his new surroundings, there was an off-kilter, dreamlike quality to what he was seeing. The sight of the deputies in the cell, the homeless woman sipping a Coke at a desk, and the ADA, a woman in a business suit clutching the handle of her slim briefcase like it was a life preserver only made it seem more surreal.

Charlotte stood beside the prosecutor and watched Wade with a mix of wariness and amusement.

He trudged past them to his desk, where he'd dumped all the junk food that they'd bought that night, and picked out a Milky Way bar, which he unwrapped as he turned to face his guest.

"May I help you?" he asked.

"I'm assistant district attorney Pamela Lefcourt and I am here to tell you that you are way, way out of line." She pointed to the cells. "I'm ordering you to release those deputies right now."

Wade took a bite out of his Milky Way bar and nodded to Charlotte, who got up and unlocked the cells. Just the taste of the chocolate and caramel seemed to clear his head, though he knew he was one long blink away from sleep.

Lefcourt took a step toward him. She was in her thirties, her dark suit perfectly pressed, her silk blouse open just enough to show a trail of freckles leading into her cleavage. Her hair was pulled back tight, making her face look even more severe than it already was.

"What the hell were you thinking arresting them?"

"I was thinking that abducting people off the street of one city and transporting them to another against their will is kidnapping."

"You are meddling in matters so far above your pay grade they are in a galaxy far, far away."

"Way, way and far, far," Wade said. "My, my."

He took another bite of the Milky Way bar as the deputies, smirking at Wade, gathered their weapons from where they'd been left on Charlotte's desk.

"I don't appreciate your attitude," Lefcourt said.

"You ought to. I'm letting these boys walk out of here as a courtesy to you," Wade said. "But I will arrest anybody I see dumping people here."

"You have no authority to do that."

"I think I do. But if you like, we can go talk to a judge about it. I'm sure bringing me back into a courtroom to discuss illegal activities by law enforcement officers won't create too much attention," Wade said. "Or maybe I'll just follow your example and start ferrying our homeless out to the suburbs. I hear the parks are big and beautiful out there."

Lefcourt's cheeks turned bright red and her nostrils flared. He allowed himself another look at her freckled chest. There was a blush there too. He wasn't entirely sure if she was furious or having an orgasm.

"I'm going to call Chief Reardon about this," she said.

"Please do." He finished off the candy bar, but the slight sugar rush was no match for his fatigue. "Be sure to give him my best."

She marched to the door, the two deputies following her. Wade watched her go, yawned, and without saying a word to Charlotte, headed upstairs to go back to sleep.

He closed the door, got onto his mattress, and pulled the bedding over his head to shield his eyes from the daylight. As he lay there in his dark cocoon, he caught Mandy's scent on the mattress and all his troubles seemed to drift away, taking his consciousness along with them.

———

Wade awoke on the floor, the sheets twisted tightly around him, the phone ringing again. He was less groggy this time when he answered.

"Yeah?"

"You were right," Billy said.

"About what?" Wade checked his watch. It was 3:00 p.m.

"Our first call is a corpse," he said.

Wade was instantly alert and sat up straight on the floor. "Where are you?"

"Outside the gates of the old King Steel factory," Billy said.

"Don't move. I'm on my way."

He hung up and called the dispatcher, asking her to send the paramedics, homicide detectives, the medical examiner, and a forensic investigation unit to the scene.

Wade put on his uniform, hurried down the stairs to the station, and grabbed the keys to a squad car from his desk drawer.

He drove out of the parking lot, got out of the car, locked the gate behind him, and then flicked on the lights and siren as he sped off.

Wade didn't use the siren because he was in a hurry and needed to clear a path in the traffic ahead of him. He did it to attract attention, to let people know that the police were there and responsive. He wanted the community to get accustomed to the sound and draw some security from it instead of fear.

He got to the factory in less than five minutes.

Billy's car was parked on the street, blocking the gate into the desolate, weed-choked parking lot. He sat on the hood, warily eyeing a dozen men who stood outside a bar across the street, watching what was happening, which so far was just the breeze fluttering the yellow crime scene tape that encircled the rusted hulk of a stripped Honda Accord in the parking lot.

Wade parked beside Billy's car and got out. Billy was idly fingering the scorched hole in his shirt.

"What have we got?" Wade asked.

"A dead woman," he said. "She's in that car."

Wade nodded. Billy seemed a bit dazed, either because he'd been shot by his boss or because he had just seen his first corpse or maybe a combination of the two. It was understandable.

"Who called it in?"

"The birds," Billy said.

"Excuse me?"

"I was cruising by and saw all these squawking crows swarming that junker," Billy said. "I was curious what the birds were so interested in. I found out."

"Did you touch anything?"

Billy shook his head.

Wade slipped on a pair of rubber gloves from his pocket and walked slowly over to the junked car, surveying the cracked asphalt and clumps of weeds for evidence. There were lots of bottle caps, broken glass, and fast-food trash around, but he doubted that any of it came from the killer. The flock of crows watched him warily from their perch on the fence twenty yards away.

The Honda had been picked clean by human vultures years ago, leaving only the metal skeleton to rot away, used as a toilet by every man and four-legged animal that passed it.

A young woman, in her late teens or twenties, was splayed out on the exposed coiled springs of the backseat, her bare feet sticking out of the open door. He didn't see a purse, wallet, cell phone, or her shoes.

She was dressed in an elbow-length cropped cardigan sweater over a V-neck T-shirt that didn't quite cover her stomach and a pair of denim mini-shorts not much larger than panties. Her feet were soft and clean, just like her hands. Her nails, on both fingers and toes, were manicured and polished.

All of that told Wade that she wasn't a street person. She had a home and probably a job.

Her skin was pale, as if she'd completely bled out, but Wade didn't see any large wounds that would account for that much blood loss. Her hair was matted with dried blood from a gash on her scalp, just above her forehead, and there was some light spatter on her clothes, but that was it. There were no large bloodstains on her clothes and no visible blood in the car.

Her left leg was swollen, blue, and bent at an odd angle, as if she had an extra joint between her knee and her hip. The flesh around her thigh was blue-black and engorged. Her arms, legs, and face were covered with divots pecked out by the crows.

She wasn't a woman anymore. She was carrion.

Wade had been at this long enough to know where all the blood had gone and what had probably killed her. But that didn't put him much ahead of the game, which was OK. This wasn't his crime to solve.

He heard a siren and turned to see a paramedic unit heading their way.

"Why did you call them?" Billy asked. "There's nothing they can do for her now."

"She's not officially dead until a medical professional says so, even if her head is across the street."

"What do you think happened to her?"

"Someone dumped her here after she was hit by a car, or took a beating, or had a bad fall," Wade said. "Whatever happened, she died from internal bleeding."

"If it's internal," Billy said. "How can you see it? You got X-ray vision?"

"Did you see her leg?"

"Yeah," Billy said, grimacing with disgust at the memory.

"She broke her femur, a sharp edge or a bone shard punctured an artery, and she bled out into her leg," Wade said. "That's why it's all bloated and blue, while the rest of her is so pale."

"I thought she was pale because she's dead," Billy said.

"The thigh can hold a lot of blood," Wade said.

"I don't want to know how you know that."

"You learn a lot of things you don't want to on this job," Wade said.

The paramedic truck pulled up behind Wade's squad car, and two guys in their twenties who looked like they hadn't slept in days got out. They put on their gloves as they approached the officers.

"What've we got?" one of the paramedics asked. His hair was disheveled and his face was covered with stubble that looked like tar.

"The body is in the car over there," Wade said. "Be careful, it's a crime scene."

"This isn't our first day on the job," Stubble-face said and went over with his partner to take a look. He leaned over her body and did a cursory check of her vital signs, and they came back to Wade. "She's very dead."

"Internal bleeding," Billy said.

"You think?" Stubble-face said.

Billy nodded sagely. "Thighs can hold a lot of blood."

Wade sighed and turned to the paramedic. "I just need an MT slip and you can be on your way."

Stubble-face reached into his back pocket for a pad that resembled a traffic ticket book. He quickly filled out a medical treatment form, tore off the top copy, and handed it to Wade.

"Have a nice day," the paramedic said.

"You too," Wade said.

The paramedics left. Billy watched them go. So did the dozen people across the street.

"What now?" Billy asked.

"We secure the scene until the homicide detectives get here."

"How long is that going to be?"

"Another ten or fifteen minutes," Wade said. "Forensics might take as long as an hour if they are stretched thin. Then it's out of our hands."

"So we're basically just guarding a corpse."

"Pretty much," Wade said.

Billy sighed. "Still beats standing at the door of a Walmart checking receipts."

CHAPTER FOURTEEN

They were still waiting an hour later for someone to show up.

The crowd on the street had doubled, even though all there was to see was two cops leaning against a police car.

"I'm impressed by your coply intuition," Wade said. "Most rookies wouldn't have stopped to check out the car."

"I don't have coply intuition," Billy said.

"You stopped, didn't you?"

"I was bored and wanted to stretch my legs."

"Coply intuition," Wade said.

Billy shrugged. "If you say so."

"You did a good job securing the scene too," Wade said. "I almost feel guilty about shooting you."

"You shouldn't," Billy said. "I'm glad to know what taking a hit in the vest feels like. Now I'll be prepared when it happens again."

"That's the right attitude," Wade said, checking his watch again.

"But if you're really torn up about it, you can buy me a new uniform shirt."

"Done," Wade said and got on the radio to the dispatcher. He requested an estimated time of arrival on the homicide detectives and was told that they were busy in the field. He asked when the forensics unit and the medical examiner would arrive on the scene and was told they were also busy and would be indefinitely delayed.

Wade clicked off and glanced back at the stripped Honda. The woman's pale foot was sticking out of the open door.

"Whoever she is," Wade said, "she doesn't deserve this."

"Deserve what, Sarge?"

"More cruelty and disrespect than she's suffered already," he said.

Wade went back to the scrapped car and began walking slowly around it in an ever-widening circle, looking for evidence and drawing a rough map of the crime scene in his notebook as he went along.

———

Another hour passed. The crowd across the street had tripled in size. Some people were even sitting on folding chairs as if they were watching a sporting event. But all there was to watch was two cops standing outside an abandoned factory doing absolutely nothing.

On the other hand, Wade supposed it was probably the first time in decades that anybody had seen cops stand around, out in the open, on a street in Darwin Gardens for two hours without getting killed.

That was something to see.

"I feel like I should start singing or something," Billy said, looking at the people. "Maybe stand on my car and give a speech. It's like they are waiting for the show to start."

Or the killing, Wade thought.

He stepped out of Billy's earshot and made a call on his cell phone.

"Homicide, Shrake," a detective answered in the stiff, no-non-sense tone common among all police officers.

"Hello, Harry," Wade said.

There was a long silence. Wade imagined Shrake debating with himself whether to hang up or not. But curiosity got the better of his former partner, who gave in with a long, bone-weary sigh.

"What do you want, Tom?"

"I've been reassigned to a community substation in Darwin Gardens."

"I heard," Shrake said.

"I'm down here now, sitting on a dead woman."

"Yeah," Shrake said. "So?"

"I've been sitting on her for two hours and nobody has shown up."

"What's that got to do with me?"

"She didn't die from natural causes, Harry. She's broken up bad and it didn't happen here. Someone is trying to cover their ass. It's a homicide case."

"Maybe it is, maybe it isn't. We'll wait for the medical examiner's report before we jump to conclusions."

"You've got to be kidding me," Wade said.

"She could have fallen out of her window or thrown herself in front of a bus and some Samaritan dragged her body out of the way and didn't stick around to get involved. Any number of things could've happened."

"And you won't know until you investigate," Wade said. "Isn't that what you do?"

"A lot of people get themselves killed in this city in all kinds of ways, not all of them criminal. We have limited resources. We've been told to prioritize."

"You'd be all over her case if her body was found in Meston Heights."

"But it's not," Shrake said.

"What happened to you, Harry?" Wade asked. "You used to be a cop."

"I still am," Shrake said. "And unlike you, I'd like to remain one."

Shrake hung up.

Wade called the medical examiner's office and asked the man who answered when they were coming.

"We can't make it," the medical examiner said. "Have the body transported to the morgue by ambulance when the detectives are done and I'll get to it when I can."

The ME hung up.

Wade stood there, shaking with rage.

It had been more than two hours since the body was discovered. It was clear now that the homicide detectives weren't coming. The medical examiner wasn't coming. And Wade assumed the forensics unit wasn't going to show up, either.

It would be dark soon.

Enough was enough.

Wade marched over to Billy. "Go back to the station. I bought some plastic sheeting. Bring me a roll, some more evidence bags, some empty moving boxes, and a box cutter."

Billy drove off. Wade went to the trunk of his car and took out his camera and a large case containing his evidence collection kit.

He began by photographing everything within the perimeter of the police tape from a variety of angles. He'd moved on to photographing the corpse when Billy returned.

Wade turned as Billy approached and he saw that the crowd had swelled even more, people arriving in cars to catch the show. One of the cars was Fallon's Mercedes, parking on a side street, giving whoever was behind the tinted glass a clear view of the crime scene.

But Wade couldn't worry about getting shot right now. There was too much he had to do and not enough time to do it.

"Billy, I want you to position your car so the headlights and spots are aimed on the scene—we'll be losing the light soon," he said. "Then I want you to start bagging and tagging whatever you see on the ground. Photograph everything before you pick it up."

"Isn't that what the forensics guys are supposed to do?"

"Yes, it is," Wade said and began dusting for fingerprints on the gate.

For the next forty minutes, the two officers silently and methodically gathered evidence, working quickly against the clock and the setting sun. Wade dusted for prints on the car carcass until the only illumination he had left came from the headlights on the squad car.

It was dark. It was time to give up.

In a little over an hour, they'd managed to take a couple hundred photographs and fill two moving boxes with bagged items and dozens of fingerprint slides.

They put the boxes in the trunk of Wade's squad car and pulled down the yellow tape around the crime scene.

All that was left now was the woman's body.

Wade picked up the roll of plastic sheeting. He'd bought it to protect the floors while he painted the station walls. But the sheeting had other purposes too. He unfurled it over the backseat of his squad car and cut the sheet from the roll with a box cutter. Then he walked over to the junked car and rolled out another sheet of plastic beside it, Billy watching him as he worked.

"I need you to give me a hand," Wade said.

"With what?"

"We're going to lift the body out of the car and place it on the plastic sheet on the ground."

"This isn't right, Sarge," Billy said.

"I couldn't agree more," Wade said, angling himself into the car.

The woman's body reeked, not so much from early decomposition as from the postmortem evacuation of her bladder and bowels. Her body was stiff with rigor mortis.

Wade placed his hands under her shoulders, Billy took her legs, and they eased her out onto the plastic sheet.

"Now what?" Billy asked.

"I want you to go back to the station," Wade said. "Before you send the photos to headquarters, make copies for us and print them out. Stay put with Charlie until I get back. If anything comes up, you go with her. I don't want either one of you going out alone."

"Where are you going?"

Wade bent down, slid his hands under the plastic, and lifted the body up in his arms.

"I'm delivering the body," he said.

Illuminated by Billy's spotlights, Wade faced the crowd on the street like an actor on a stage as he carried the corpse to his car and laid her down gently on the backseat.

When he rose again, he looked at the crowd. Everybody he'd met so far was there. Claggett, Terrill, Friar Ted, and Mrs. Copeland. Timo and the crew who'd trashed his Mustang. Mandy and her father.

And Duke Fallon, the window rolled down in his Mercedes so Wade would see him and know that he was there.

Friar Ted, clutching a tattered Bible, crossed the street and approached Wade.

"May I?"

Wade nodded. Friar Ted peered into the backseat, swallowed hard, then recited a blessing, the Lord's Prayer, and a psalm, then leaned forward to make a cross on her forehead, but Wade stopped him before he could touch the corpse.

"Thank you, Padre," Wade said.

"No, thank you, Sergeant." There were tears in Friar Ted's eyes.

Wade got into his car and drove away.

———

There were no hills in Meston Heights. The only elevation was a social one, an aura of wealth and power the developer had conjured up in 1910 as an advertising ploy to add prestige to what otherwise would have been just one more tract of subdivided ranchland.

As a marquee, and to bestow class on the patch of dry dirt, the developer built an outrageously ostentatious gateway modeled after the Arc de Triomphe, only on a much smaller scale, and stuck a big fountain with a marble nymph in front of it.

The initial homes behind the gateway were architecturally diverse but uniformly grandiose in square footage and pomposity, establishing a template that still endured to this day.

The Spanish Colonial home on Mantley Drive evoked the style of an old California mission, with its red-tiled roof and towers, monumental wood door, and the arched, covered balcony that ran along one side of the house.

Wade laid the woman's body on a plastic sheet on the front doorstep and placed the boxes of evidence down beside it.

And then he got back into his squad car and called Police Chief Gavin Reardon on his private office line.

"Yes?" the chief answered.

"Good evening, Chief," Wade said. He could hear the hum of conversation, some piano music, and the clatter of dishes. The chief was at a restaurant or perhaps attending a party. "It's Tom Wade."

"How did you get this number?"

"Roger gave it to me," Wade said. "For emergencies."

"You're on your own down there," the chief said. "I thought I made that very clear."

"Oh, you did," Wade said. "Nobody cares about the crime in Darwin Gardens unless it shows up on their doorstep."

"So why the hell are you calling me?"

"Because it just showed up on yours," Wade said. And then he hung up.

CHAPTER FIFTEEN

When Wade got back to the station, he found Charlotte at Billy's desk, the two of them sorting through the crime scene photos.

"Thanks for sticking around, Billy," Wade said. "You can go home now."

"What did you do with the body?" Billy asked, getting up from his seat.

"He took it to the morgue," Charlotte said irritably. "Where else do you think he'd take it?"

Billy shrugged and glanced at Wade, who took his seat and began going through the photos. Wade had to give the kid credit. Billy's instincts were sharp. It was an encouraging sign. The kid might actually become a decent cop if he learned to trust his gut.

"You did some real good police work today," Wade said.

"Thanks," Billy said. "It was fun."

"Fun?" Charlotte asked. "A woman was murdered."

"What are you mad at me for? I didn't kill her," Billy said and walked out the back door to his car.

Wade found a close-up of the dead girl's face and studied it. People who died a natural death often looked to him like they were sleeping. But he found that it was seldom true when a person was killed. There was no peace in their final expression.

He looked at Charlotte. "What happened to that homeless woman that we brought in last night?"

"I offered to drive her to a women's shelter on my way home," Charlotte said. "But she asked me to take her back to Lincoln Park, so I did."

"You weren't worried about running into the deputies we arrested or maybe some of their friends?"

"It didn't even occur to me," she said.

It was a gutsy move. Or a stupid one. But the same could be said of many of the things that he did.

"I'm sure Billy filled you in on everything. So what are your thoughts?"

"I think that you committed multiple violations of department protocol in your handling of the crime scene," she said. "It's not going to make things easy for the prosecutors when this case gets to court."

"You're assuming that this crime will be solved and that someone will be tried for it."

"We always have to," she said.

"I feel the same way."

"So you're telling me that's why you did what you did," she said.

"Yes, I am."

"I think there's more to it than that."

"That's because your father is a shrink," he said.

"Probably," she said and gestured to the photo of the victim in his hand. "Do you have any idea who she is?"

"No, but I'm going to find out. Let's eat before we roll. I'm buying."

He led her to the front door, locked it behind them, and walked across the street to the Pancake Galaxy. A hush fell over the twenty or so customers in the restaurant as the two cops came in. The loudest sound was Peter Guthrie's wheezing.

Wade recognized many of the faces from the crowd at the crime scene. He nodded in greeting and made his way to the counter with Charlotte, where they settled onto the stools and picked up menus.

"What do you recommend?" she asked.

"Pancakes and apple pie," he said.

"That's an unusual combination," she said.

He shrugged. "It's tasty."

Mandy Guthrie came out from the kitchen balancing several plates of food on her arms. She smiled the instant she spotted Wade, which made him smile too.

"Be right with you, Tom," Mandy said.

She went off to deliver the food. Charlotte looked after her, then back at Wade, who perused the menu.

"Tom?" Charlotte said.

"That's my name."

"She seems glad to see you."

"Then we must be making progress," Wade said.

"Is that what you two are making?"

He didn't comment, and tried to remain expressionless, as if he hadn't heard what she'd said. But it was obvious to him now that he might have underestimated both of his rookies.

Mandy returned, stood across the counter from them, and held out her hand to Charlotte.

"I'm Amanda Guthrie. My friends call me Mandy." She tipped her head toward her father, who was sniffing the smoke from the cigarette smoldering in his ashtray. "That's Peter, my dad."

"Officer Charlotte Greene," she replied.

"What can I get you?" Mandy asked.

Charlotte ordered a salad. Wade ordered a cheeseburger and a slice of apple pie. When Mandy went back to the kitchen, Wade told Charlotte about the special neutral, protected status the restaurant seemed to have in the neighborhood.

"This helps," Pete said, lifting up Old Betty from behind the counter.

Mandy brought out their food and, after attending to a few other customers, poured herself a cup of coffee and hung out at the counter with them while they ate.

Wade's cheeseburger was as great as the pancakes. He was beginning to understand why everyone in Darwin Gardens shared a common interest in keeping the Pancake Galaxy safe and in business.

"Everybody is talking about you again today," Mandy said.

"What are they saying?" he asked.

"They can't figure you out."

"They aren't alone," Charlotte said.

Mandy dismissed her remark with a wave of her hand. "He's easy to understand. It's accepting it that's hard for some people."

"So did you set them straight?" Wade asked.

"Hell no," Mandy said. "That's your job."

The bell over the front door rang, indicating that a new customer was coming in. Mandy looked past Wade and immediately went rigid.

Charlotte swiveled around on her stool to follow her gaze and saw Duke Fallon coming in with Timo behind him. Fallon was wearing another tracksuit, his sleeves pushed up to show off the Rolex on one wrist and the gold chain on the other.

"Is the pie as good as I said?" Fallon asked as he came up and stood behind Wade and Charlotte.

"Not quite," Wade said.

"I guess it depends on who you're fucking." Fallon glanced at Mandy before shifting his gaze to Charlotte. "Pardon my French."

"*De rien*," Charlotte said.

"What's that?" Fallon asked.

"French," Charlotte said.

Fallon gave her an icy smile. "Did you read your horoscope this morning?"

"I don't believe in astrology," Charlotte said.

"Neither do I, but it's something to read while I'm taking a crap. Your horoscope predicted that you and Wade would be badly hurt today. But here you two are, feeling no pain."

"My back is a little sore," Wade said. "Does that count?"

"That's what happens when you engage in rigorous activity with your lower back," Fallon said, giving Mandy a look. She looked right back at him. "My point is, what the moon and the stars tell you don't mean shit here. You know why?"

"Because it's ridiculous to think that the alignment of the planets impacts human behavior?" Charlotte asked.

Fallon looked her in the eye. "Because I control the universe on these streets, honey."

"How much control do you have over this?" Wade took the photograph of the dead woman out of his shirt pocket and set it faceup on the counter next to his pie.

Fallon glanced at it. "I saw you out at the factory today, cleaning up the mess."

"That wasn't what I was doing," Wade said.

"Then what were you doing?"

"I was processing the crime scene and gathering evidence."

"Why would you do that?"

"Because a woman was murdered, Duke, and I'm going to arrest the son of a bitch who did it."

"You are?" Fallon asked.

"I am," Wade said.

"What the hell for?"

Wade tapped the photograph with his finger. "Her."

Mandy turned the picture around and looked at it. "Do you know who she is?"

"Not yet." Wade picked up the picture and held it out to Fallon. "Maybe you know somebody who does."

"Maybe." Fallon took the picture from Wade and stuck it in his pocket. "What about the other women?"

"What others?" Wade asked.

"The crack whores. Maybe five or six the last couple of years. I didn't see anybody processing the crime scene and gathering evidence for them," Fallon said. "The only time I've seen that happen before down here is when the bodies on the ground were cops."

"Things have changed," Wade said. "I live here now."

"Maybe that's why your horoscope didn't come true today," Fallon said. "But you never know what will happen tomorrow."

He smiled at Charlotte, acknowledged Pete with a respectful nod, and walked out of the restaurant with Timo.

Wade turned back to his plate and took a bite out of his pie.

"Do you know anything about other women being murdered?" Wade asked Mandy.

"No, but people get killed here all the time," she said. "Most of them for crossing Duke Fallon."

"Makes me wonder why he's inviting me to investigate," Wade said.

"Maybe he's daring you to," Charlotte said.

"It's not that," Pete said, his voice raspy. "Duke grew up here. This is his home. Nobody wants to find a corpse in their front yard."

Wade worked on his pie and mulled things over for a few moments. Neither one of the women minded Wade's silence. Charlotte had some thoughts of her own to consider, and Mandy had customers to serve.

After a time, the bell rang over the door again.

The new customer was a heavyset woman in her late forties with bloodshot eyes, tear-streaked cheeks, and a large mole under her left ear. She walked up to Wade. She was shaking.

"My name is Ella Littleton," she said, her voice almost a whisper. "The girl you found, her name is Glory. She's my daughter."

CHAPTER SIXTEEN

They took Ella to a booth in the back, got her a cup of coffee, and began by asking her for basic details, like her address and phone number, and her family history.

In Wade's experience, going over the dull, mundane details had a calming effect on emotional individuals and helped them focus.

Ella told them that she'd lived in Darwin Gardens all her life. She and her three children lived in a bungalow in Belle Gardens, a few blocks from Mrs. Copeland's place. Her children each had a different father, none of whom stuck around, which she saw as a blessing, since they were all shitbags, anyway.

She got by on welfare and by doing laundry for single men in the neighborhood she called "useless trash too dumb to know how to wash their own socks," not unlike her own sons.

"Glory's older brother is in prison for armed robbery. Her younger brother is in the gangs, so it's only a matter of time before he's in prison himself or in the dirt. But Glory isn't like them," Ella said, sitting across from Wade and Charlotte, who took notes. "She's a good girl. A hard worker. Cleaning houses in Havenhurst every day and offices downtown every night."

"When did she leave the house yesterday?" Wade asked.

"I don't know, maybe eight. She took the bus to clean for the Burdetts. They're rich folks, good people, bought her some nice clothes so sometimes she can work at their parties."

"But you don't actually know if she did or not," Charlotte said.

"I heard her leave, but I didn't get up," Ella said. "I wish I had."

"When does she usually get home?"

"After she's done cleaning the offices, around midnight," Ella said. "But she didn't come home last night."

"Has that ever happened before?" Charlotte asked.

Ella gave Charlotte a hard look. "She always comes home. She's a good girl."

"I'm sure she was," Wade said. "But even good girls have boyfriends."

Ella shook her head adamantly. "I told you, Glory is a good girl. She was getting out. She wasn't supposed to die here."

She looked down into her coffee cup and started to cry.

Wade decided not to press Ella any further for now. He could circle back to her later if he needed more information. So he expressed his condolences and promised to do everything within his power to find out what happened to her daughter.

The two officers got up and walked out, leaving her with her sorrow.

———

Wade let Charlotte drive again. It gave him more time to think.

"Did Fallon tell Mrs. Littleton to talk with us?" Charlotte asked.

"She wouldn't have spoken to us without his OK. I get the feeling nothing goes on down here without it."

"Except the women getting killed," Charlotte said. "Do you think he really cares about them?"

"I know he cares about his authority being ignored and the message it sends if he lets anyone get away with it."

"The same could be said about you."

"Maybe that's why Duke and I get along so well," Wade said.

A yellow taxicab sped past them in the opposite direction, heading toward downtown. The light on his roof indicated that he had a fare, but his backseat appeared to be empty.

"He's speeding," Charlotte said.

"I don't blame him," Wade said.

"It's brazen," she said. "He sped right by us and we're the police."

"The law says he has to accept a fare to anywhere in the city. But now that he's dropped off his passenger he wants to get out of here alive and with all of his money."

"So we aren't going to give him a ticket?"

"Nope," he said.

"Maybe we should give him a police escort out of the neighborhood."

"That would be overkill," he said.

"Glad to know we're drawing the line somewhere," she said.

Something fluttered at the edge of his peripheral vision. He looked out the windshield and saw a woman staggering across the road, right in front of their car.

Wade yanked the steering wheel hard, sending the car up onto the sidewalk, narrowly avoiding the woman.

Charlotte slammed on the brakes and they stopped, a few inches short of hitting a streetlight, the car straddling the asphalt and the sidewalk.

Wade bolted from the car and rushed over to the woman. She was in a hospital gown that was hanging open in the back, exposing her naked, bruised body. Her feet were bare, calloused, and dirty, her knees scraped and bleeding. She was easily in her sixties and, from the looks of it, a homeless person.

"Ma'am?" Wade asked. "What happened to you?"

She looked through him as if he weren't there. "Here, kitty-kitty. I've got tuna for you."

Wade waved his hand in front of her eyes. She noticed him now.

"Yes, I'll supersize that," she said.

Charlotte joined him. "Should I call for a paramedic?"

Wade gently took the woman's right hand and examined a yellow plastic band around her wrist. There were some numbers on it, the day's date, the name "Jane Doe," and the name of the hospital.

"No," Wade said. "We're taking her to Community General ourselves."

"Blake Memorial is closer," she said. "Community General is at least ten miles from here."

"But just a short cab ride away," Wade said.

He led Jane slowly by the arm back to the squad car and helped her into the backseat.

Community General was on the north end of town, where downtown slowly dissolved into Crescent Heights, a recently gentrified neighborhood of restored Victorian homes, small cafés and boutiques, art galleries, and several prestigious interior design and architecture firms.

The hospital was saved from bankruptcy and the wrecking ball by community activists eager to preserve its art deco architecture and to ensure that an urgent-care facility would continue to serve their neighborhood. Wade suspected that their idea of urgent care was a collagen injection to puff up a lip before a date.

The entire way there, Jane Doe babbled incoherently about grout, Pat Sajak, watermelon seeds, flatulence, and a hundred other things.

They pulled up to the ambulance entrance. Charlotte got out, found a wheelchair, and brought it to the car, and Wade helped Jane into it.

Wade marched into the ER and Charlotte wheeled Jane in behind him.

The ER looked more like an Apple Store than a hospital, all the surfaces gleaming and white, aglow from hidden lights. Flat-screen monitors and high-tech devices that Wade didn't recognize were everywhere. The staff's lab coats and scrubs all fitted as if they'd been tailored by fashion designers.

The young nurse at the front desk had the smile of a stewardess and the body of a fashion model. Her smile became a scowl when she saw Jane.

"She's back already?" the nurse asked.

"You know this woman?" Wade replied.

"This woman doesn't know this woman," the nurse said. "She's cuckoo for Cocoa Puffs."

"Then why did you release her?" Wade asked.

"You'll have to ask Dr. Eddington," she said and paged the doctor.

The doctor arrived a few moments later. His hands were in the pockets of his lab coat, his silk tie perfectly knotted, his sparse comb-over covering his bald spot with surgical efficiency. His eyes narrowed behind his octagonal glasses and his face puckered into a scolding sneer as he caught sight of Jane.

"Oh God," Eddington said. "When will you people learn?"

"Which *people* are you referring to?" Charlotte asked tightly.

"You people," Eddington said, waving his hand at Wade and Charlotte. "This is a hospital, not an elder-care facility."

"She needs medical attention," Charlotte said.

Jane bolted up from her wheelchair. "From Miami Beach, it's *The Jackie Gleason Show!*"

Charlotte gently eased her back into her seat.

"She's had medical attention," Eddington said. "You people brought her in here three days ago. Apparently, she took a tumble in Riverfront Park. Her injuries were minor, nothing more than simple scrapes. We treated them and waited for someone to show up to claim her."

"She's not a piece of baggage," Wade said.

"We made every effort to locate family or friends," Eddington said. "And you people were no help. In the meantime, we fed her, cleaned her, and gave her a bed for three days. When she asked to leave, we had no authority to keep her."

"You could have had her committed," Wade said.

"She seemed perfectly lucid at the time."

"Like she is now," Wade said and gestured to her. Jane was playing a make-believe violin and humming to herself.

"She wasn't a danger to herself or to others," Eddington said.

But she was to the hospital's bottom line.

Community General had barely avoided bankruptcy once already, so Wade was sure that the employees were under enormous pressure to cut costs. The staff knew that they would never be reimbursed for the medical care she'd been given or the bed that she'd occupied. They didn't want to risk the potential of any further costly involvement with her that might arise from committing her to a mental institution. And since no one seemed to care about her anyway, there was a simple, low-cost solution to their problem.

"So you called her a cab," Wade said.

"I even paid for it out of my own pocket," Eddington said. "As a courtesy."

"Aren't you sweet," Charlotte said.

Eddington shot her a nasty look.

"Where did you tell the cab to take her?" Wade asked.

"I didn't," Eddington said. "I gave the cab driver thirty dollars and figured that would take her wherever she wanted to go in King City. You'd have to ask her where she told him to go."

Eddington turned to walk away. Charlotte stepped in front of him, blocking his path. "Where do you think you're going?"

"Back to work," Eddington said. "I've got patients."

"And she's one of them," Charlotte said, pointing at Jane. "She's suffering from some kind of dementia."

Eddington snorted. "So now you people are doctors as well as police officers?"

Charlotte got right in his face, their noses practically touching. "If you call us 'you people' again, you're going to need a fucking doctor."

Wade bit back a smile.

"We are a hospital, *Officer*," Eddington said tightly, taking two steps back from her. "We are not an Alzheimer's treatment facility or an old-folks home."

"The law requires you to make arrangements for post-release care before discharging any patients," Charlotte said. "We didn't find any medications or paperwork on her."

"Obviously, she lost them," Eddington said.

"Here's what I think," Wade said. "You stuffed a senile old woman wearing nothing but a hospital gown into a cab and told the driver to dump her in Darwin Gardens instead of back in Riverfront Park so she'd be Blake Memorial's problem if anything else happened to her. You didn't want to incur any more costs. The mistake you made was forgetting to snip off her wristband."

Eddington shot an involuntary glance at the nurse, who immediately looked away. She was in for some hell once Wade left. The doctor focused his attention back on Wade.

"She wasn't ill, she asked to leave, and we discharged her," Eddington said. "What you think is irrelevant."

"She was staggering through the streets, incoherent and disoriented, and was nearly run over, which makes her a danger to herself and to others. So you're going to take care of her." Wade stepped close to Eddington and lowered his voice to a whisper that only the doctor could hear. "And if you abandon her in Darwin Gardens again, I'll pick you up, put your naked ass in a hospital gown, and leave you there too."

Wade turned and walked out. Charlotte followed. They got into the squad car and they sat there for a moment in silence, Wade in the driver's seat, thinking things through.

Darwin Gardens had become the city's dumping ground for unwanted souls—whether they were homeless, criminal, delusional, or in his case, disgraced.

Wade knew it was why he was there, and Charlotte was smart enough to know that's why she was too. There was no place for a smart, liberal, African-American woman in Chief Reardon's department. Billy was probably the only one who didn't know why he was there.

It gave Wade and Charlotte, and even Billy, a kinship with the people in Darwin Gardens. They were all discards.

"My mom is a lawyer," Charlotte said. "I'll ask her to look out for that old lady."

"She'd do that?"

"She would for me," Charlotte said.

"You can't make it personal every time you meet someone who needs help," Wade said.

"It's just this once," she said.

"It's your second day," Wade said. "You're going to see more and you're going to see worse."

"Aren't you optimistic," she said.

"I'm just saying that it's possible to care too much in this job."

"It's better than not caring enough," she said, glancing back at the emergency room.

On the way back to Darwin Gardens, they stopped at a hardware store so Wade could buy some motion-activated outdoor floodlights.

While he was inside, Charlotte called her mom, who agreed to represent Jane Doe, and she talked to her father, the shrink, who offered to do a psychiatric evaluation of the old woman and have her committed to a mental hospital for treatment if it was necessary.

Charlotte told him all of that once he returned to the car. *How convenient*, Wade thought. *One-stop service for the needy, the homeless, and the senile.* He wondered how many times she'd make that call in the next few weeks and when her parents would finally stop answering the phone.

She motioned to the outdoor lighting that he'd bought.

"What's all that for?" she asked.

"Mrs. Copeland," he said, and then told her about arresting Terrill in the alley. "I'm going to swap her the bullhorn for the lights and install them over the alley. It will keep the junkies away."

"Aren't you the same man who just told me not to make it personal every time I meet someone who needs help?"

"It's only a couple of lights."

"You're right. It's nothing," she said. "It's not like you're moving into her neighborhood."

They drove back to the station in silence, Charlotte smiling to herself. She knew she'd won that round and that Wade knew it too.

CHAPTER SEVENTEEN

Wade could see that something was wrong before they reached the curb in front of the station. The sidewalk was sparkling, the glow of the streetlight reflecting off thousands of glass shards.

He got out of the car and looked around. The Pancake Galaxy was closed, the lights off. There wasn't a single person on the streets.

He walked up to the station, the glass crunching under his feet, and surveyed the damage.

The front windows were shattered, except for a few large, jagged panes either still clinging to the frame or caught between the wrought iron bars.

The counter had taken the brunt of the assault, shielding the computers on the desks and other equipment from damage. But there were bullet holes everywhere.

Charlotte stepped up beside him, her hand on her holstered gun, ready to defend herself.

Without a word, he unlocked the front door and went straight for the gun locker, opened it up, and removed a shotgun. He returned to Charlotte, handed her the weapon, and locked up the station again.

"What are we going to do?" she asked.

"What has to be done," he said wearily.

Wade drove straight to Headlights in silence and parked out front. There were half a dozen cars in the parking lot and nobody on the street. He kept the motor running.

"Get behind the car and cover me." He grabbed the shotgun and got out. She got out too.

"Whatever you're about to do, I'm sure we shouldn't be doing it," she said as they passed each other in front of the car.

"It's the only thing we can do," Wade said. "Are you ready?"

"For *what*?"

"To back me up if people come out shooting," he said.

She took her position behind the car, drew her weapon, and nodded. But he could see that she was frightened. It was one thing to draw your gun on a shooting range at paper targets, another on the street against real people.

Wade turned, raised his shotgun, and aimed it at the neon sign shaped like a naked woman. It struck him as a unique piece of sleazy Americana that added a bit of character to the neighborhood. It was a shame to lose it.

He pulled the trigger, blasting the sign apart in a shower of sparks and broken glass.

The front door of Headlights flew open, and Wade spun around, aiming his shotgun into the six furious men who stood there, fronted by Timo, who was already giving him his ready-for-his-close-up snarl.

"This is getting tiresome," Wade said to Timo. "How many times are we going to have this dance?"

"You are dead," Timo said.

"So you've said. You can only kill me once."

"You are *all* dead," Timo said, staring past him to Charlotte, who held her gun steady. "Duke loved that sign."

"It would still be there if someone hadn't shot up my police station," Wade said. "Think about that. Duke will."

The snarl on Timo's face faltered.

"Everybody back inside," Wade said. "And close the door behind you."

They did as they were told.

"You're driving," Wade said to Charlotte.

She holstered her weapon and quickly got into the car. He backed up, his gun trained on the door, and got into the car. The instant he was inside, Charlotte sped off, peeling rubber.

"Slow down," Wade said. "You're making it look like we're fleeing."

"What you just did was totally illegal," she said, practically yelling at him. It was the adrenaline. "You could lose your badge for that."

"You think they're going to report me?" Wade asked.

"I might," she snapped.

"Do whatever you think is right," he said.

"I would, but I don't want lose my fucking badge on my first fucking week on the fucking job."

It seemed to Wade that whenever Charlotte got really angry, she was stricken with a mild case of Tourette's syndrome. He found it endearing.

"That's a sticky dilemma," Wade said.

She glared at him. "You've faced off with that guy before, haven't you? It's how you got all of those guns you had me take downtown."

"He shot my car, so I shot his."

"My God," she said. "You're behaving like children."

"We can't afford to look weak," Wade said, "or we will never establish our authority."

"Don't worry," she said. "You'll be dead long before that becomes an issue."

"It was just a threat," he said.

"This tit-for-tat game can only escalate," she said. "It won't end well."

Wade knew she was right, but he also knew that there was no other way. Someone had to quit. Or die. It was how things were, and always had been. Evening the score was the oldest brand of justice that there was, and in the absence of any other kind, it was better than nothing.

It eventually restored the balance, which was a kind of peace.

An imperfect peace, but peace nonetheless.

They went back to the station and swept up the glass without speaking a word to each other. There was nothing they could do about boarding up the space left by the windows until morning.

After a snack of candy bars and coffee, they went back on patrol, cruising around the neighborhood in silence and without trouble until daybreak, when they returned to the station.

Wade got in his Explorer and drove to a lumberyard. He bought several sheets of plywood, strapped them to the roof of his car, and went back to the station, where Charlotte was using a knife to dig the bullets out of the front counter and drop them into evidence bags. It was pointless, but the right thing to do.

Wade began hammering the plywood over the windows inside the station while Charlotte busied herself with the latest issue of *American Police Beat*. She was pissed off and not hiding it well. He was nearly done with the job when Mandy walked over with two cups of coffee and surveyed the damage.

"It doesn't look like you're making a lot of friends around here," she said.

"At least I've made one," he said, taking the coffees from her.

"Yeah, but you can't sleep with everybody."

Wade looked over his shoulder to see if Charlotte heard the remark, but if she had, she wasn't acknowledging it.

"Thanks for the coffees," he said.

"I'll put them on your tab," she said and walked away.

Wade brought one of the coffees over to Charlotte and set it down on the desk in front of her as a peace offering and retreated to his desk.

They were still sipping their coffees in silence when Billy drove up, doing a slow glide as he passed the front of the station, then parked in back. He bounded in already in uniform and full of energy and enthusiasm. It made Wade feel all the sleep he wasn't getting. He had to get more rest, but that would have to wait until he made some progress that day into Glory's murder. He knew from experience that the best chance of closing a homicide is within the first forty-eight hours. After that, the chances of solving it drop dramatically. He couldn't afford to sleep.

"Holy shit," Billy said. "What happened?"

"We had a drive-by last night," Wade said.

"I wish I could have been here last night to back you up," Billy said. "I've never been in a shoot-out."

"There wasn't one," Charlotte said. "We weren't even here when it happened."

"It was a warning," Wade said.

Charlotte got up and dropped her coffee cup in the trash. "I'm out of here."

"You're that scared?" Billy asked her.

"No, I'm that tired," Charlotte said. "My shift is over, remember? I'm going home."

"On your way, I'd appreciate it if you'd stop by MTA headquarters and get the security-camera tapes from all the Blue Line buses that ran to Havenhurst on Monday."

"You think you'll see Glory on one of those tapes?" Charlotte asked.

Wade shrugged. "Either way, it'll tell us something."

"Who is Glory?" Billy asked.

Wade tossed Billy a set of keys. "The dead girl. I'll tell you all about it while you drive."

"Where are we going?"

"Havenhurst," Wade said.

"That's not on our beat," Billy said.

"It is today," Wade said.

———

Havenhurst was one step higher up the social ladder than Meston Heights. For one thing, there were actually a few hills there, all of them offering spectacular views of the Chewelah River. But the best properties were right on the river itself or along several man-made tributaries. They all featured huge mansions set back from the water by an acre or two of lawns, pools, gardens, guesthouses, and tennis courts.

The Burdett house was an English Tudor perched on a hill that sloped gently down toward the river, where they had a large matching Tudor boathouse and dock.

Wade parked the squad car in the cobblestone motor court beside a sparkling Bentley and a new red Ferrari.

The two officers got out. Wade turned to Billy, who was admiring the Ferrari as if it were a *Playboy* centerfold.

"Stay here," Wade said.

"Gladly," Billy said and stroked the hood of the car.

Wade went to the front door of the house, where he was met by a big-haired blonde woman in her fifties in a V-neck blouse and shorts. The angles on her face were unnatural, her lips were too plump, and her skin was too taut, all of which combined to make her look constantly stunned and ready to kiss something. She stepped out onto the porch, her big, hard breasts leading the way.

"May I help you, Officer?" she asked.

"I'm Sergeant Tom Wade. Are you Gayle Burdett?"

"Yes, I am," she said. "Are you looking for a donation to the policeman's ball?"

"I didn't know we had a ball," he said.

"It's at the Claremont, down on the water, in the fall. It's lovely. It raises all kinds of money for the department."

"I've never been invited."

"Maybe you haven't sold enough raffle tickets to earn an invitation."

"That must be it," he said. "Actually, I'm here about Glory Littleton."

Gayle stepped aside and gestured for him to come inside. "What has she done?"

Wade edged past her breasts into a grand marble foyer with two large sweeping staircases that framed the entry to the two-story great room and picture windows with an incredible view of the lawn, the dock, and the river. "What makes you think that she's done anything?"

"You're here, she didn't show up to clean yesterday, and she's one of them."

"Them?"

"Those people down there," she said, waving her hand in the general direction of downriver. "You know who I mean. The ones who will pimp their mother for crack."

"Oh yeah, *those people*."

"But she's always been great with us," Gayle said. "I could leave my jewelry out when she was dusting and not worry about a thing. Was I wrong?"

"She didn't commit any crimes—at least not that I know of."

"So what's the problem?"

"She's been murdered," Wade said.

Gayle gasped and put a hand over her mouth. Her eyes were already very wide, so he was grateful for the gasp—otherwise, he wouldn't have been able to detect any shock or surprise on her face.

"Oh my God," she said. "The poor girl. Ethan needs to know."

She took a deep breath to calm herself, then marched off behind her chest. Wade followed, noting that her ass had been reshaped to match her breasts, or perhaps it was vice versa. She looked like she had a pair of basketballs implanted front and back.

Gayle led him through a kitchen, which was large enough to run a restaurant, and on through the dining room, which was large enough to entertain a government, and then out through a set of French doors to the brick patio, which was large enough to hold a high school graduation.

There was another grand stairway, this one outside and made of stone, that spilled onto a cobblestone path that led down to the dock, where Ethan Burdett was in their twenty-foot, vintage-style, mahogany-and-fiberglass runabout, leaning over the side and scrubbing a black smudge off the gleaming, piano-key-white hull with a rag.

Ethan was in his fifties and tennis-court fit, wearing a white yacht skipper's cap, polo shirt, chinos, and Top-Siders without socks. Wade wondered if the attire was a legal requirement of boat ownership.

Unlike his wife's, Ethan's tan was natural, rather than applied, and the closest he'd been to a plastic surgeon was writing one checks. Wade thought Ethan would be a perfect actor for one of those Cialis ads, the ones that always ended with both couples sitting naked in separate his-and-hers bathtubs in a rainforest.

Gayle spoke up, her voice shaking. "Ethan, I have terrible news."

Ethan glanced at Wade and assumed the worst. "Oh shit, which one of our cars did my son total this time? Tell me it's not the Porsche."

"It's about Glory," Gayle said. "She's been killed."

Ethan blinked hard, took off his hat, and sat down on one of the pleated leather seats that matched the color of the hull. "Jesus. What happened?"

"She left home to clean your place and ended up dead and dumped at the King Steel factory," Wade said. "Did either of you see her yesterday morning?"

"I was stuck in an arbitration all day with a room full of lawyers," Ethan said, then glanced at his wife. "Did you see her?"

Gayle shook her head. "She never showed up. I tried calling her cell, but she didn't answer. I was furious about it. The house looked like such a dump after the weekend and we had the Wittens coming for dinner. I had to do the cleaning myself."

Wade glanced back at the dump. It was a palace compared to anything in Darwin Gardens or even the tract-home sprawl of New King City.

"When did Glory start working for you?"

"About a year ago," Ethan said. "She was part of the crew that cleans up my office at night. I was impressed by her work ethic and her positive attitude. She really wanted to make something of herself and I wanted to help her attain that goal."

Gayle wiped a tear from her wide eyes. "I was cursing her all day for not showing up, and all that time, God only knows what horrors were being inflicted upon her. I am such a bitch."

"Don't be so hard on yourself, honey," Ethan said. "Think instead about all the good things you did for her. We enriched her life in so many ways. You treated her like another member of our family. We all did."

"Really?" Wade said. "So how many of your relatives clean your toilets and take a bus home to Darwin Gardens every night?"

Gayle stiffened up, pulling her shoulders back and aiming her breasts at Wade as if they were cannons. They certainly looked like they were loaded with large cannon balls.

"Are you implying that what happened to Glory is our fault for not inviting her to live under our roof? Maybe we should invite the gardener and the pool man to live with us too."

"He knew what I meant," Ethan said to his wife, then stood up and faced Wade. "I'd like to know why a simple patrolman is asking questions about a homicide. Isn't that a job for a detective?"

"Yes, it is," Wade said. "And the fact that I'm the one who's here proves that Glory isn't being treated like a member of your family at all."

He turned and walked away.

CHAPTER EIGHTEEN

There was an Escalade parked in the motor court beside the Bentley. The SUV was tricked out with lots of chrome and a custom front grill of silver mesh.

Billy was admiring the Escalade with a guy in his twenties wearing a muscle shirt to show off his arms, board shorts, and flip-flops as Wade quietly came around the side of the house.

The guy wanted everybody to see his arms, not because they were muscled, but because he had the Twenty-third Psalm tattooed in small but flowery script on one and some Chinese letters and the comedy and tragedy theatrical masks on the other.

"This is a nice ride," Billy said, admiring the Escalade almost as much as he had the Ferrari. "Love the chrome."

"I did it myself," the guy said.

"No shit? I've got a 'sixty-eight Chevy Impala convertible that I'm fixing up."

"You ought to come down to my body shop. I'll cut you a deal."

Billy was about to reply when he noticed Wade standing a few feet away. He immediately stiffened up.

"I appreciate the offer, but I don't accept any special consideration," Billy said. "I only go full freight."

The guy noticed the shift in Billy's tone of voice and followed the officer's gaze to Wade.

"I've got a 2008 Mustang that's taken a beating," Wade said, approaching them both. "Maybe I'll stop by too."

"Please do. Tell all your friends." The guy reached into his pocket, came out with two business cards, and handed them out. "Have 'em ask for Seth Burdett. I own the place."

Wade pocketed the card. "Aren't you worried that having a bunch of cops around your shop will cut into your business from Darwin Gardens?"

Billy blinked hard, no doubt wondering how Wade had made that leap. He wouldn't have wondered if he'd seen Timo's matching Escalade.

"I have clients from all over King City," Seth said. "Talent gets noticed. Word gets around."

"Was it Glory who spread the word for you down there?"

"How do you know Glory?" Seth asked.

"I don't, but I'm trying to," Wade said. "Might help me figure out who killed her."

Seth staggered back as if he'd just absorbed a blow and hugged himself. Wade cocked his head and read a portion of the psalm on Seth's arm:

Yea, though I walk through the valley of the shadow of death,
I will fear no evil:
For thou art with me;
Thy rod and thy staff, they comfort me.
Thou preparest a table before me in the presence of mine
enemies;
Thou anointest my head with oil;
My cup runneth over.

At least Seth didn't need to look any farther than his arm to find comfort.

"What happened to her?"

"We don't know. Her body was in Darwin Gardens. It looks like she took a bad beating or maybe was hit by a car. Maybe it happened there, or maybe someplace else. Did you see her anytime on Monday?"

Seth shook his head. "I was out on the interstate all day, doing my community service, picking up trash on the shoulder."

"You're on probation?"

"I've only got sixty-eight hours left, if I don't throw myself in front of a big rig first from the sheer fucking boredom."

"Hey," Billy said, "it beats jail."

"I wanted to do the time, to have that raw experience, but my dad wouldn't let that happen. His fucking lawyers got me out. I only stayed for a few hours. It wasn't even down in county, just the King City Central Lockup."

Wade shared a look with Billy, then shifted his gaze back to Seth. "Let me get this straight. You *wanted* to go to jail."

"Hell yes. You don't know what it's like up here. You're cushioned from everything. Nothing is raw. How's a man supposed to get tough if nothing ever cuts, you know what I'm saying?"

"Is that what Glory was?" Wade asked. "A raw experience?"

Seth gave Wade his best death stare. Wade had seen scarier expressions on a Smurf. Maybe Seth's worries about getting too soft weren't entirely unfounded.

Wade was half tempted to suggest he spend some time with Timo working on some scary expressions when his cell phone rang. He answered it.

It was the chief.

———

Wade parked the squad car at Riverfront Park in a spot that gave them a view of the river, the King's Crossing Bridge, and if they turned their heads to the left, police headquarters at One King Plaza.

"What are we doing here?" Billy asked.

"I've got to talk to somebody. While I'm doing that, I'd like you to stroll over to headquarters, get me Seth Burdett's rap sheet, and pull the files on all the dead women found in Darwin Gardens in the last couple of years."

Billy frowned. "I want to switch to the night shift."

"Why do you want to do that?"

"Because that's when all the good stuff happens."

"You found a body," Wade said.

"That's only exciting if she's alive, looks like Megan Fox, and I find her in my bed."

Billy got out of the car and trudged off toward headquarters. Once Wade was sure Billy was out of sight, he got out and strode toward the river.

Chief Reardon stood at a picnic table, smoking a cigarette, which he flicked into the river as Wade approached.

"You wanted to see me, sir?" Wade asked.

"You've gone insane," Reardon said. "Totally bat-shit crazy."

"Is there something in particular that makes you say that?"

"You dumped a corpse at my house, arrested two deputies, and harassed one of the biggest political donors in this city. I could take your badge right now, toss it into the river, and nobody, not even the AC fucking LU would question it."

"Then, do it," Wade took off his badge and set it on the picnic table.

"That's the first sensible thing you've done in two years," the chief said, reaching for the badge.

"Of course, now I will go tell my story to anybody who will listen. You'll have to explain why you aren't investigating the murders of those women in Darwin Gardens," Wade said. "And why you're letting deputies forcibly relocate people from one part of the county to another."

Chief Reardon glared at him for a long moment, then set the badge back down on the table. "What do you want?"

"A thorough autopsy conducted today on Glory Littleton and the forensic evidence that I collected at the scene processed as quickly as possible. I'd like both of the reports sent directly to me."

"That's it?" Reardon asked. "That's *all* you want? I thought the least you'd ask for is an immediate transfer out of Darwin Gardens."

"I'm just trying to do my job," Wade said. "I don't care where I have to do it."

The chief shook his head and walked past Wade toward police headquarters.

Wade picked up his badge, shined it on his sleeve, and pinned it back on his chest.

———

Wade walked into the station around noon and was surprised to see Charlotte at her desk, fast-forwarding through security-camera video from inside a bus that she was watching on her computer.

"You're supposed to be off duty," Wade said.

"So are you," Charlotte said. "I've been watching those Blue Line tapes. Glory took the bus to Havenhurst on Monday morning, just like her mom said. But I can't find any footage yet of her coming back."

"When you're done watching that, and if you're still willing to stick around, you can help Billy go through the case files on the other women who were killed down here."

"Oh joy," Billy said as he came in lugging a box full of binders and dropped it on his desk.

"It's called police work," Charlotte said. "You should consider yourself lucky that we get to do it."

"That's the spirit," Wade said.

"What are we looking for?" Charlotte asked.

"Whatever the murders have in common and anything that they don't."

"What are you going to be doing?" Billy asked.

"Sleeping," Wade said and headed for the stairs.

With each step, he felt more and more tired.

He was on his fourth day in Darwin Gardens without an uninterrupted stretch of sleep. At some point, he knew the sleep deprivation would catch up with him. He just hoped it wouldn't be during a confrontation with an armed felon.

As soon as he got into the apartment, he undressed and stood under the shower, letting the hot water pour over him.

It wasn't only the physical exhaustion that was getting to him, but also the stress of dealing with all the political and personal forces aligned against him, not to mention the responsibility of guiding two rookie officers and getting accustomed to a new home.

He'd yet to unpack anything besides his bedding and toiletries.

It all made him feel unmoored in a way he hadn't felt before. And whenever he felt insecure or uncertain in anything in his life, he reached for the one thing he knew he could depend on.

The badge.

And everything that it stood for.

Now, standing there naked in the shower in his rat-hole apartment above a former adult-video store in Darwin Gardens, he had a minor epiphany.

His father always had a single, pat answer for every decision that he made.

What's important is what you stand for and how strong you stand for it.

It defined Glenn Wade, and now it defined his son too.

Wade finally understood why.

It was the one thing in his life that he could control. No matter what else was happening around him, that was the one thing that nothing and nobody could change, except him.

It made the world something that could be defined, managed, and understood. It had worked for his dad, out there on the lake, where life was a lot simpler and there were fewer shades of gray.

But not so well for his son in King City, where everything was political and interconnected, where corruption was in the city's DNA, where principles were seen as something malleable instead of absolute.

Except by Tom Wade.

And therein lay the problem.

What's important is what you stand for and how strong you stand for it.

Living by those words was how he held strong and never lost his way, even when the moral compass of everyone around him lost direction.

He stayed true to course and did the right thing.

And lost everything he had.

Now living by those words was all that he had left. Everything else in his life was different, but there was one thing he could be certain of and that would never change: the job he had to do and the way he had to do it.

For now, that meant enforcing the law on his beat and finding whoever was killing women in Darwin Gardens, no matter where the investigation led.

Just like when he was in the MCU.

He hoped things would turn out better for him this time around, though he'd gladly settle for justice for the dead women and mere survival for himself and his two officers.

The water had gone from scalding hot to ice cold as he'd stood there, pondering his situation. He got out of the shower, dried off, wrapped a towel around his waist, and was about to go to bed for the afternoon when there was a knock at the door.

Wade thought about putting on a bathrobe but then realized he didn't know which box it was in. The towel would have to do. He opened the door, expecting to find Charlotte or Billy standing in the hallway.

But it was Mandy.

"Are you too tired to talk?" she asked.

"Yes," Wade said and kissed her, pulling her into his apartment and kicking the door shut.

She yanked the towel from his waist and pushed him down onto the mattress.

He let himself fall.

CHAPTER NINETEEN

It was evening. They lay naked on the mattress, Mandy curled up against Wade, her head against his shoulder and one leg draped across his thighs.

"You haven't been getting much sleep," she said.

"You aren't helping."

"Is that a complaint?"

"Hell no," he said. "What was it you wanted to talk with me about?"

"This was what I wanted," she said and gave his penis a playful tug. "But if I couldn't seduce you, I was going to tell you that Glory wasn't such a good girl."

"How do you know that?"

"Because there's no such thing, except maybe in the eyes of a girl's mother. If you want the truth, you have go to her friends, which I did. They told me that Glory had a rich boyfriend in Havenhurst."

"Did they give you a name?"

"They didn't know who he was, only that Glory believed that he was going to be her ticket out of here."

"You got out," he said. "What was your ticket?"

"A vivid imagination," she said. "When I was a kid, I wrote stories about unusually clever girls who discovered portals to magical worlds in their closets or backyards and escaped into them."

"Is that what happened to you?"

"You could say so," Mandy said and rolled onto her back beside him. Her nipples were hard and her cleavage was damp with sweat. He had to control the urge to get on top of her and lick the moisture from between her breasts. "My stories got me a scholarship to Bennington, where I earned an English degree, married another wannabe writer, and moved to New York. We took odd jobs and worked on our great American novels."

"How'd that work out?" He pulled a sheet up over his waist, uncomfortable in his nakedness.

"He sold his novel, had an affair with his editor, and I walked out. Not long after that, Mom died of a heart attack and left my dad all alone to take care of himself and run the restaurant. I can write anywhere, so I came back home."

"How's the novel going?"

"I burned it." She sat up and reached for her panties.

"Stay with me awhile," he said, stroking her arm.

She stood and put on her panties. "I'd really like to, but I saw how you were looking at my boobs. We'll just end up fucking some more."

"Perish the thought," he said.

Mandy started getting dressed, stepping into her pants and pulling her shirt over her head. "Yeah, but if you get killed because you're too tired to shoot straight, it's going to mess me up sexually for the rest of my life."

"I wouldn't want that," Wade said.

He watched her dress. When she was done, she gave him a warm smile.

"See you later, Officer," she said.

"You left your bra on the floor," he said.

"I know," she said, heading for the door. "I did it on purpose."

"What for?"

"So you won't forget what you were thinking about doing five minutes ago." She winked at him and walked out.

He managed to grab a few more hours of sleep, then suited up and went downstairs. Charlotte was asleep, her head on a pile of papers on her desk. Billy was leaning back in his chair, feet up on his desk, reading a file.

Wade gently nudged Charlotte as he passed her on his way to his desk, which was still piled with junk food. "Rise and shine, Officer Greene."

Charlotte sat up, her hair flat on one side of her head, her eyelids heavy from sleep. "I'll rise, but I can't promise any shine."

Wade grabbed a bag of Cheetos, sat on the edge of his desk, and looked over at Billy while he ate. "What can you tell me about Seth Burdett?"

"He's a rich, spoiled, wannabe gangbanger covered with tats just so he can say 'fuck you' to his parents without actually saying it."

"I meant, what have you learned from his file?"

"He's the go-to guy in Havenhurst for drugs. Arrested twice, walked twice."

"I'll bet that he's getting his drugs from Timo," Wade said.

Charlotte stretched and got up to get herself a Coke from his desk. "That's a big leap."

"Not if you know that Seth chromed Timo's Escalade."

"I haven't seen it," Billy said.

"Neither have I," Charlotte said, popping the tab on her drink and taking a sip.

"That's because I gunned it down," Wade said.

Charlotte shook her head. "You sure like shooting cars."

"It's preferable to shooting whoever is driving them. It certainly cuts down on the number of wreaths I've got to send to funerals."

"You're joking, right?" Billy asked.

"What I'm wondering," Wade said, ignoring Billy's question, "is whether Timo is acting on Duke's orders or going into business for himself."

"What difference does that make?" Charlotte asked.

"I'm not sure yet," Wade said. "What did you two learn about the women being killed down here?"

"There have been seven killings in the last two years," Charlotte said, taking a seat at her desk again and referring to her notes. "All were prostitutes and drug addicts. Each one was shot in the chest at close range and left in an alley under a blanket or a flattened cardboard box."

"Was there any forensic evidence?"

"Nothing at all from the crime scenes. It's like they just picked up the bodies and ran. Semen was recovered from some of the victims, but considering how these women lived, that's no surprise. DNA testing on the samples hasn't been done and, as far as I can tell, hasn't even been ordered."

Wade's face tightened. If the victims were seven Meston Heights party girls, doing as much drugs and screwing as many guys, the DNA testing would have been a top priority.

The class disparity between who got justice and who didn't certainly wasn't unique to King City or news to Wade, but the more often he encountered it, the more it rankled.

"Anything else?" he asked, setting his bag of Cheetos aside and looking for something to wipe his hands on.

She nodded. "They were all killed with the same gun and they all had olive oil on their faces."

"Is olive oil some kind of organic moisturizer?" Billy asked. "I read that some Japanese women even put bird shit on their skin."

"What it is, Billy, is a pattern," Charlotte said, in the most patronizing tone of voice that she could muster. "A big, fat, obvious one. There's a serial killer down here and nobody is doing a damn thing about it."

"We are," Wade said.

"But the woman we found wasn't shot, covered up, or doused with salad dressing," Billy said.

"You're right. She doesn't fit the pattern. So I guess that means we're going after two killers," Wade said, finding a piece of typing paper and wiping his hands with it. The paper made a lousy napkin.

He looked up and saw Charlotte and Billy both staring at him. For once, they were both in agreement about something.

"I forgot to buy napkins," Wade said. "What do you want me to do, wipe my hands on my pants?"

"Maybe you haven't noticed," Charlotte said, "but we aren't homicide detectives."

"We're barely even police officers," Billy said.

Charlotte glared at him. "Speak for yourself."

"We're the only law in Darwin Gardens," Wade said. "So we'll have to do."

———

Mission Possible was a soup kitchen by day, but at night the tables were replaced with cots for the junkies, drunks, and transients who had nowhere else to go.

About sixty of those sallow-eyed men and women, most of them Native American, were milling around waiting as Friar Ted and some volunteers made the switchover, folding up the tables and stacking them.

Wade and Charlotte walked in and the homeless tried to melt into the shadows, only there weren't any to be found in the harsh fluorescent light. So they lowered their heads, hoping if they didn't see the cops, the cops wouldn't see them. It wasn't as childish as it seemed. Invisibility was something they rarely had to work to achieve.

Charlotte carried a folder and followed a step or two behind Wade, who greeted Friar Ted and introduced him to her.

"May we have a word with you?" Wade asked.

"Certainly." The preacher led them over to one of the remaining tables in a far corner of the former warehouse.

"That was quite a show you put on the other night," Friar Ted said.

"Just doing my job, Padre."

"Arresting cops seems to be your specialty."

"Not by choice," he said. "I need your help."

"I'll do anything I can."

Wade glanced at Charlotte, who passed the folder over to Ted.

"I have to warn you," she said. "These are disturbing images."

"That's just about all you see around here, Officer. You'll learn that soon enough." He opened the folder and looked at the morgue photos of the dead women. True to his word, he appeared unshaken by the sight.

"Do you recognize any of them?" Wade asked.

"I recognize the sunken faces of the suffering, the faithless, the damned. I see them every day."

"What I meant was, did you know any of these women personally?"

Friar Ted shook his head. "I wish I did. And I wish they could have known the glory of God."

The preacher slid the folder over to Wade, who made no move to take it.

"You can hold on to those. The killer is probably a john. I'd appreciate it if you'd show the pictures around to the women who come in here—maybe they know the guy."

"Of course," he said. "But I wouldn't be too hopeful if I were you. They aren't a very talkative group."

"I have faith," Wade said.

CHAPTER TWENTY

Wade had somewhere he wanted to go downtown, but his stomach was growling, so he made a detour first, stopping at one of the mini-marts in Darwin Gardens that he hadn't visited yet. The store had more bars on the windows than the county jail.

"What are we doing here?" Charlotte asked.

"Stopping for a snack. I skipped lunch. Or maybe it was dinner. Whatever. All I know is that I'm hungry."

"There are a dozen places we could go downtown for a decent meal."

"But that wouldn't help me build relationships with the people on our beat. I'm getting a Coke and a Slim Jim. Want one?"

"What is a Slim Jim?"

"A stick of spicy meat," he said. "You could buy it now and eat it in a year and it will still be fresh."

"You say that like it's a good thing."

"It is if you leave food in the cupboard as long as I do," he said.

"I'll pass, thank you."

"Are you sure?"

"I've never been more sure of anything in my life," she said.

Wade shrugged, got out of the car, and strode into the mini-mart. It was like all the others in Darwin Gardens—cramped and garishly lit, with narrow aisles that were overstuffed with items. The front counter was cluttered with impulse-buy candy and snack displays.

The guy behind the counter was his thirties, lanky and unshaven, with an enormous head of tangled hair and a faded T-shirt. He forced a smile.

"Hello, Officer, what can I get for you?"

"I'm looking for Slim Jims," Wade said.

"Over there." He gestured in the general direction of the rear of the store, which was an odd thing to do, since there was an assortment of Slim Jims on the front counter.

"Thanks," Wade said and knew in that instant that he wasn't going to make it downtown tonight, that what he'd wanted to do would have to wait until tomorrow.

He picked up a basket and headed purposefully down the aisle to the glass refrigerator case in the back, which was full of beer and soft drinks.

Wade slid open the glass door and grabbed a liter of Diet Coke, stealing a glance up at the round mirror mounted in the corner, near the ceiling.

The mirror was angled so that the clerk could see if anybody was shoplifting in the back of the store. But it also allowed Wade to see the storeroom door that was behind him and to his right.

The door was ajar, held open by the toe of someone's scruffy tennis shoe.

At that moment, all that existed in Tom Wade's world was that mini-mart, the guy at the counter, and whoever was in the storeroom.

Wade unscrewed the cap from the bottle of Diet Coke, took a sip out of it, and then stuck the open bottle in his basket as he made his way to the candy aisle. He picked up a roll of Mentos mints and a few other candy bars, dumped them in his basket, and then headed back to the register.

He set the basket down on the counter. "I couldn't find the Slim Jims, so I made do."

"Sorry," the cashier said. "We must be out."

Wade began unwrapping the Mentos as the cashier rang up his items.

"That's funny," Wade said. "What are these right here?"

As the cashier leaned over the counter to look, Wade dropped a Mentos into the open bottle of Diet Coke, which burst into a foam geyser that blasted into the man's face.

In the same instant, Wade whirled around and drew his gun, aiming it at the storeroom door. "Do you want you want to die tonight?"

"No, fuck, no," someone said behind the door.

"Drop your weapon and step out with your hands behind your head." Wade took a step back so he could keep his eye on the drenched cashier at the same time. "You too, hands up."

Wade heard something metallic hit the floor in the storeroom and then the door opened. A man came out. He was thin and jittery and sweating from every pore, his hands on his head.

Charlotte rushed in now, her gun drawn and pointed at the Diet Coke–doused man behind the counter. "Don't move, stay right where you are."

"Is there anyone else with you?" Wade asked.

"No, it's just us," the man behind the counter said.

She covered the two men while Wade, his gun still drawn just in case, went to the storeroom and slowly pushed open the door the rest of the way with the toe of his shoe. Inside, he saw an old man sitting on the floor, his mouth sealed with duct tape, his hands bound behind his back, a gun on the floor at his feet.

Wade kicked the gun aside and carefully removed the tape from the man's mouth.

"Was it just them?" Wade asked.

The man nodded.

"Are you OK?"

"Yeah," the man said. "I'm used to it. Those two assholes came in, pointed a gun at my face, and said they'd let me keep my brains if I didn't make trouble. I didn't get this old being stupid. A week doesn't go by that I don't get robbed by somebody."

"Those days are over. I owe you $2.99 for a liter of Diet Coke and a buck for a roll of Mentos. Don't let me forget." Wade turned back to Charlotte. "Cuff 'em and read 'em their rights."

She did.

They took a report from the shopkeeper, then drove the two robbers back to the station and locked them up while Charlotte filled out the necessary paperwork.

Wade used the time to start patching some of the holes in the walls left from the shelves, the posters, the firebombing, and the drive-by shooting.

At daybreak, he went upstairs for a quick, two-hour nap, showered and shaved, and put on a pair of jeans, a T-shirt, and a Windbreaker. He came back down to the station to find a sour-faced Billy waiting for him at Charlotte's desk.

"I am definitely switching to nights next week," Billy said. "I haven't had to draw my gun once yet, and she's got to three times."

"I've been meaning to ask you about that trick with the Mentos," Charlotte said. "It wasn't something we were taught at the academy. Where did you learn it?"

"*America's Funniest Home Videos*," Wade said.

"I can't picture you watching that show," she said.

"My daughter did," Wade said. "In fact, this is my day with her. So here's what's going to happen while I'm gone."

Wade told Charlotte to transport the two robbers to the lockup downtown and to take the patrol car home with her. He showed Billy where the patching and painting materials were and told him to stick around the station and work on the walls.

"What does that have to do with being a cop?" Billy asked.

"It's about showing your pride for your profession, among other things. It's why firefighters keep their trucks as shiny as jewels."

"But I don't know how to paint," Billy said.

"It can't look any worse than it does now," Wade said. "The important thing is, I don't want you going anywhere while I'm gone."

"I went on patrol before, remember?"

"That was before the drive-by," Wade said. "I don't want you out there alone right now."

"What if an emergency call comes in?"

"It'll be a trap," Wade said. "Nobody calls the police down here. Not yet, anyway."

Wade told Billy to call him if anything came up and then headed out in his rented Explorer for the suburbs of New King City.

As he drove across the Chewelah River on the King's Crossing Bridge, passing the familiar landmarks of what was once his daily commute, he felt as if he were awakening from a bad dream. The closer he got to Clayton, the suburb where he'd lived, the farther away and less real Darwin Gardens became.

By the time he pulled into the driveway of his house, he could almost believe none of it had ever happened—the corruption of the MCU, the trial, his divorce—and that it had just been one miserably long drive home.

He got out of his car and stood in the driveway for a moment, looking down the street of tract homes. Everything seemed cleaner and more colorful, as if the sun somehow shined brighter here. The air was tinged with the fragrance of flowers and freshly mowed grass instead of exhaust fumes, puke, and dried pools of urine. The asphalt was black and smooth instead of gray and riddled with potholes. There were no bars on the windows, no graffiti on the walls, no used condoms and syringes in the gutters.

Paradise.

Being back in New King City again, he could understand the temptation to haul away any transients who showed up here, to do whatever was necessary to prevent this place from becoming the one he'd just left. It would be a crime to let this become Darwin Gardens, especially while his family still lived here.

But intellectually, he knew that the rot that crept into the once prosperous south side, eventually turning it into Darwin Gardens, wasn't carried like a plague by the wandering homeless. It was far more complicated and insidious than that.

The future of these suburbs, the safety, beauty, and cleanliness that made them so desirable, had more to do with the continued economic survival of the New King City tech companies than anything else. All it would take was a few of those employers shutting down and outsourcing their business to India or China, putting thousands of the heavily mortgaged owners of these tract homes out of work, and New King City could quickly become Old King City.

He turned toward the house and saw Alison standing on the front walk, studying him.

"You're looking at the street like you've never seen it before," she said.

"Maybe I haven't," he said. "At least not the way that I do now."

Alison looked beautiful, and he felt a sudden, and painful, longing to hold her. And with that longing, he felt guilty for having been with another woman. The guilt made no sense, of course, since they were divorced. But ending the marriage wasn't his idea. He'd gone along with it because it was what she wanted. If she changed her mind now, he'd come back to her with no hard feelings, as if the divorce had never happened.

She tipped her head toward the Explorer. "What happened to your car?"

"It's in the shop, having some body work done. I had a little accident."

"Are you OK?"

"Just fine," he said.

"You don't look it."

I suppose I should look terrific after losing my family, my home, and my career and starting over as a beat cop in the worst corner of King City. That's what he thought, but it wasn't what he said.

"I'm not getting enough sleep lately."

"Brooke tells me you're back on the force," she said.

He nodded. "It's not the same job, but it's the same pay, rank, and benefits."

"That's good," Alison said, putting her hands on her hips, letting Wade know that trouble was coming his way, "but I would have appreciated hearing about the job from you rather than my daughter."

"I'm sorry," he said. "I didn't plan it that way. Things were hectic and Brooke caught me off guard."

"You haven't learned a thing," she said. "So I guess you gave up on the idea of going into private security."

"That was your idea, Ally, not mine."

"The department must have offered you something great to keep you from the private sector. What did they do, make you the head of the MCU?"

"They put me in charge of a community substation in Darwin Gardens."

She stared at him in shock. "That's a hellhole."

"Pretty much," he said.

"Don't you see what they're doing? It's retribution, Tom. They are trying to humiliate you or, more likely, get you killed for what you did."

"That's not how I see it," he said.

"I'll remember that at your funeral," she said. "Next month."

"The job gives me a salary that allows me to support my family, pay the mortgage on this house, and still have a little bit left over to take care of myself. It also comes with a health plan that will cover Brooke's orthodontia, among other things. I can't do that working campus security at a college."

"But that's not why you took the demotion."

"Lateral move," he said.

"Whatever." She kept staring at him.

"No," he said. "It's not."

She shook her head with disappointment. "We're divorced, but that doesn't mean that I've stopped caring about you, Tom. I'd make whatever sacrifices I had to—I'd sell this house without a second thought—if it would keep you from taking a job that's suicide to pay our bills. But there's nothing I can do to save you from your own twisted sense of honor."

That's when Brooke came out of the house, marching up purposefully behind her mother. She was tall and thin like her mother, with a runner's slim, muscular legs and long hair tied in a ponytail that fell almost to her waist.

There was an adorable band of freckles across her nose and cheeks that gave her a huggable cuteness that was dramatically undercut by the mature intensity of her brown eyes, narrowed now in a stony gaze. Wade could see himself and his father in that gaze, and he was pretty sure that Alison could too.

"I hope you two aren't fighting again," Brooke said.

"We're not," Alison said. "I was just telling your father that I'm concerned about him."

"I am too," Brooke said. "You look terrible, Dad."

"So I've heard," he said. "But you know what would really help?"

"Two Advils and some concealer?"

"A big hug and a kiss," Wade said and crouched down so she could run into his open arms. She groaned at the request because he was treating her like a child, but she gave him what he wanted, hugging him tight and kissing him on the cheek.

"I know you won't take the makeup," Brooke said into his ear, "but I would still recommend the Advil."

He looked over her shoulder at Alison. "I'll have her back by dinnertime."

"There's no hurry," Alison said. "It's not a school night."

"Yeah, but I've got the night shift," Wade said.

"Of course you do," she said. "I'll bet that you even volunteered for it."

"I assigned it to myself," he said.

"Of course you did," she said, turned her back to him, and walked into the house.

CHAPTER TWENTY-ONE

Thirty minutes later, sitting in a crowded theater at the Clayton Commons shopping center, he wished that he'd followed Brooke's advice and taken those Advils.

The movie Brooke dragged him to was one of those big-budget comic book adaptations where good-looking people in colorful costumes tried to work out their superficial super-angst by throwing cars at each other and making as much noise as possible.

It gave Wade a splitting headache. He closed his eyes, which seemed to help, and it put him right to sleep. Wade slumped down in his seat, spilling the kernels and crumbs that remained at the bottom of his popcorn bag all over his lap.

Brooke wasn't offended by her father napping through the movie. He'd obviously needed the rest and she was glad just to be with him. But she was thankful that his snores were drowned out by the cacophony of super-heroic destruction, sparing her embarrassment if any of her friends happened to be in the audience.

She nudged him awake over the closing credits. He blinked hard, sat up in his seat, and rolled his head to work out a kink in his neck.

"Sorry that I fell asleep," he said, wiping the crumbs off his lap. "Are you mad at me?"

She shook her head. "I'm glad you slept through the movie. It made it a lot less awkward for me to watch the blow-job scenes."

"Shhh," Wade said, looking around. "I know there weren't any sex scenes in this movie because superheroes don't have sex. They fly around instead. And you shouldn't be using words like that."

"Like blow job?" she said, smiling with amusement.

"It's not something thirteen-year-old girls should be saying."

"But there are plenty of thirteen-year-old girls giving them."

"I hope you're not one of them."

"I'm not. I'm just saying that asking me not to use the word doesn't mean that I don't know about oral sex or that you're protecting my innocence."

"I know that, believe me. I see the harsh realities of life every day. But you were just using the word for shock value."

"And it worked," she said. "You're wide-awake now."

They walked out of the theater into the Commons, a shopping center designed to look like a quaint European village that just happened to be in the middle of Washington State.

The center was a bizarre mishmash of architectural cues—a Danish windmill atop a pharmacy, a German half-timbered facade on a grocery store, an Italian café facade on a Subway franchise, and an assortment of French *colonnes*, stand-alone pillars topped with onion-shaped iron domes that displayed wraparound advertising for things like discount bikini waxes.

Wade and Brooke went for lunch at Panda Express, which had a Spanish-Moorish facade, and sat at a table outside, facing a small lake filled with ducks and a three-story Big Ben replica with an enormous Rolex clock face that was the centerpiece of the Commons.

The center was remarkably clean, and the pressed concrete sidewalks, made to look like aged but inexplicably shiny cobblestones, gleamed in the afternoon sun.

"Where do you live?" Brooke asked.

It was a topic he'd been hoping to avoid, especially with Alison, though he knew he couldn't evade the issue for long. But he needed time to settle in and then figure out the best way to present it to the two of them.

"I'd rather talk about you," Wade said.

"Besides my parents splitting up, and having my first period, my life hasn't changed much," she said. "I live in the same house, I go to the same school every day, I get good grades, and I often wonder what's happening with my dad."

"You can call me anytime," he said.

"The same goes for you," she said. "But I'm always the one who calls."

"I've been busy and distracted, that's all. I miss you very much. The hardest thing for me to live with has been not coming home to you each night and having breakfast with you every morning."

"But at least you can picture what I'm doing," she said. "What my world is like, where I am, what I am up to. I can't even do that because I don't know where you are or who you're with."

Brooke wasn't going to let go—Wade could see that now. She'd always been stubborn and tenacious, but something had changed about her since the divorce. It seemed to Wade that she saw him in a different, more objective way, apart from him being her father.

Whenever they got together now, she seemed to be taking his measure, comparing the man he was to the man she thought she knew. And she was discovering his flaws.

Those changes were probably a natural part of growing up, but he wondered if the divorce hadn't sped things along a bit. It would be foolish to assume that the divorce, not to mention the trial and the media frenzy that surrounded it, hadn't changed some of her attitudes about him.

Wade decided that she deserved straightforward answers to her questions, regardless of the difficulties or discomfort it might cause for him now.

"I'm working in a tiny precinct in Darwin Gardens," Wade said. "And I live in an apartment in the same building."

Her eyes went wide. "Why would you want to be there?"

"Because that's where I'm needed most."

"But it's not safe," she said.

"That's why they need me," he said. "To make it safe."

"Wouldn't you rather be somewhere like this?"

He looked out at the fountains with their jets set in time to the Sinatra standards playing on hidden speakers, at the French statuary imported from a crumbling chateau in Bordeaux, and at the security guards rolling around on their futuristic Segways.

"Not really," he said. "There's not much use for a cop here."

He was about to look back at his daughter when something else caught his eye: a shiny Escalade with distinctive custom chrome work and tinted windows.

"OK," she said, "but why do you have to live there?"

"I have to live somewhere," he said, shifting his gaze back to his daughter.

"There are other places you can live that are a lot nicer and far less dangerous than Darwin Gardens."

He'd let his guard down driving out to New King City. He wouldn't let that happen again.

"I'm sure that there are. But I'm trying to send a message to the people there." Sitting across from her now, he felt a circle being closed. He remembered a Saturday afternoon he'd spent fishing on Loon Lake with his father, who told him roughly the same thing that he was about to tell her. "What's important is what you stand for and how strong you stand for it. I can't think of a better way of showing it than making their home mine too."

She studied him for a long moment and then nodded. "Neither can I."

He'd assumed she'd throw more questions at him, that she'd challenge his decision and try to reason with him. But instead, he got simple acceptance and understanding, something he never knew that he needed or wanted from her. It was a jarring realization for him to discover that he did and that he was thankful for it.

Wade wondered how she would interpret the code that he'd lived by, how she'd shape it for herself, and how she'd pass it on to her children. He hoped that, unlike his father, he'd be around to see it.

"I'm glad that you understand," he said, reaching down as if to scratch his leg, but using the move to unsnap the strap holding his gun in his ankle holster.

"You'll make that point to them even stronger when you bring me there on the weekends."

Her comment took him completely by surprise. He sat back in his chair, shaking his head, literally distancing himself from the idea.

"No way," he said. "It's not safe for you there."

"I'll be with an armed police officer," she said. "How much safer could a citizen of King City possibly be?"

"It's too dangerous for you there now, especially with a cop at your side," Wade said, glancing again at the Escalade in the parking lot. "It's what I'm trying to change, but that's going to take some time and maybe some bloodshed before it happens."

"Are there families in Darwin Gardens?"

"Of course there are," he said.

"Do they have kids?"

"Of course they do," he said.

"So what you're saying, and what you're standing for now, is that you're a cop who can't even protect your own kid, much less the ones who live there. You can't say it any stronger to them, or to me, than by being too afraid to bring your own daughter home."

On one level, he admired the intelligence of Brooke's argument and how deftly she'd boxed him into a corner with his own words. He was proud that she wasn't doing it over something trivial and childish, like wanting to get her belly button pierced, but rather, over a matter of principle and her desire to be with him.

But the very thought of bringing her to Darwin Gardens terrified him, overshadowing whatever pride he felt over how she'd argued her case.

"I'll think about it," he said, but he knew that he wouldn't have to. As soon as Alison heard where he was living, and was pissed off about getting important family news from Brooke rather than from him yet again, she would certainly forbid him from taking his daughter to his new place.

It would make Alison the bad guy with Brooke and not him, but that was the only upside. He'd still end up with both women furious with him. Brooke for not fighting Alison's decision and Alison for once again being the last to know about Wade's decisions.

Wade didn't wear his Kevlar vest in Darwin Gardens, but he thought he might have to start wearing it to visit his family.

"Good," she said and excused herself to go to the restroom. He used the opportunity to get up and walk over to the Escalade. Seth Burdett must have worked overtime to repair it.

Timo rolled down the window. He was alone in the car. "Your daughter looks soft. Would you like me, maybe a few guys I know, to break her in for you? I think she'd like that."

"If I see your face here again," Wade said, "I'll put a bullet in it."

"You won't see me." Timo grinned. "But she might."

Wade started to turn, as if to go, then lashed out his fist so fast that Timo didn't see it coming until it made contact with his nose, smashing it like an egg.

Timo toppled, stunned, over his center console, blood all over his face. Wade reached inside, took the keys from the ignition, then grabbed Timo by one ear, pulling him close.

"Listen up, dumb shit," Wade said, his voice barely louder than a whisper. "You pull anything up here and it won't be about me anymore. You'll bring total Armageddon upon Darwin Gardens. The entire police force will march in and decimate it. But before that happens, I'll find you, jam my gun so far up your ass you can lick it, and then I'll blow your head clean off."

He released Timo, tossed the keys into a gutter, and walked back to the restaurant just as his daughter was coming out again.

"Who were you talking to?" she asked.

"An Indian with a broken nose," Wade said. "You ever see him hanging around, you let me know right away."

She looked past her father to the Escalade but couldn't see anyone behind the tinted glass.

"Why?" she asked. "Is he dangerous?"

"Not as much as I am," Wade said, putting his arm around his daughter and leading her away.

CHAPTER TWENTY-TWO

The wedge-shaped glass office tower, at the corner of Grant Street and McEveety Way, stood on the original site of what had been McEveety's General Store in the frontier days, the hub of commerce and gossip for the area's settlers, farmers, and ranchers.

Vincent McEveety was one of the four founders of King City, and the third incarnation of his store on that property, a two-story brick-and-stone structure, had survived well over a century after his death from liver disease.

The general store grew over time in size, if not influence, and became McEveety's Department Store in the early 1900s, which it remained until it was sold in the 1960s to the Cartwell's chain, which ran it until they went under in the 1980s.

Over the following fifteen years, the building housed many different businesses, none of them lasting long, and decayed with the neighborhood around it.

When developers, supported by the city, proposed tearing down the building and replacing it with an office tower as part of an ambitious upscale revitalization and gentrification of McEveety Way, several citizen groups banded together and blocked the move in court, hoping to delay the project while they tried to have the building declared historically significant.

The opponents were making headway, getting support from all over the state, but before the matter could be legally resolved, the building and most of the city block were destroyed in a massive gas explosion. The cause of the leak, and what ignited it, was never determined, despite an initial determination by investigators that it was arson. The rubble was cleared, and McEveety Tower, named in honor of the historic building that it replaced, went up within a year.

Wade figured McEveety, a ruthless developer himself, would have appreciated the fate of his store and seen the tower, and the victory of commercial interests over historical preservation, as a far more fitting memorial to him, and the values of King City, than his old building.

The fourth floor of McEveety Tower was occupied by Burdett Shipping, which was what brought Wade and Charlotte there late that Saturday night, though Wade had intended to come the previous evening before getting sidetracked by the mini-mart robbery.

They strode into the marble lobby and up to the circular burled-walnut front desk, where an old security guard with a pear-shaped head sat in the center, watching the monitors embedded in the counter in front of him.

The guard looked up as Wade approached and immediately broke into a smile of recognition.

"I'll be damned. Tom Wade." The guard stood right up and eagerly shook Wade's hand. "After what you did, I thought for sure that you'd be someplace where the sun don't shine."

"I am," Wade said, then gestured to Charlotte. "Officer Greene, this is Sam Appleby, retired watch commander at McEveety station, where I started out."

"Pleased to meet you," Charlotte said.

Appleby shook her hand.

When Wade worked with Appleby, he was all muscle and sinew, without an ounce of body fat. But he'd put on weight over the years, and now it was all yielding to gravity. Everything on Appleby seemed to be sagging toward his feet. Maybe that was why Appleby sat right back down again.

"I had no idea you were back on your old beat," Wade said. "What happened to the dream of spending your days fishing at Deer Lake?"

"It's a vacation when you do it two weeks a year. It's a new kind of hell when it's your life."

Apparently, Appleby had forgotten that Wade grew up on a lake.

"This is better?" Wade asked.

"At least now I enjoy fishing again," Appleby said. "How'd they get away with busting you down to uniform?"

"Technically, it's a lateral move."

"You could have walked," Appleby said, then waved his hand in front of him, as if dissipating smoke. "Never mind, I forgot who I'm talking to. So what brings you here, Tom?"

Wade handed Appleby a picture of Glory Littleton.

"Ah hell," Appleby said. "She was such a sweet girl. I heard she'd been killed. What happened?"

"That's what I'm trying to figure out. Did you know her?"

"Nothing beyond pleasantries," Appleby said. "I saw her each night when she came in and four hours later when she left. But I'd keep my eye on her until she got on the bus."

"She lived in Darwin Gardens," Charlotte said. "How much danger could she be in on a street where Gucci, Louis Vuitton, and Armani have their stores?"

"She's dead, isn't she?" Appleby asked.

"Was she here on Monday?" Wade asked.

Appleby shook his head. "She didn't come in."

"Did she have a locker here?"

Appleby grabbed a key ring from the desk, hit a button that electronically locked the lobby doors, and got up. "Follow me."

He led them across the lobby to an unmarked door, which he unlocked and that opened to a corridor with linoleum floors, white walls, and bars of fluorescent lights along the acoustic-tiled ceiling.

"No marble and chandeliers for the help," Charlotte said.

They followed Appleby into a windowless room with a scuffed-up table in the center surrounded by mismatched plastic and folding chairs. There was a vinyl couch repaired with duct tape, some vending machines, a refrigerator, a sink, a microwave, a utility closet, and a wall lined with gym lockers that looked like they'd been recovered from a junkyard. A maid's cleaning cart, stuffed with supplies, dusters, brooms, and a vacuum, was parked in a corner.

"Welcome to the employee break room, though nobody hangs out here. They grab their lunches and go outside. The maids keep their uniforms in here and change in the restroom across the hall." Appleby stepped up to one of the lockers and knocked a knuckle against the tin. "This was Glory's."

"You got a key for it?" Wade asked.

"Nope. But the handyman's closet is over there and I'm going on break."

Wade and Appleby shook hands, and then the security guard walked out. Charlotte watched him go, a look of confusion on her face.

"What was that supposed to mean?"

"He was saying we don't need a key," he replied, walking over to the closet, opening the door, and peering inside.

"We still need a search warrant."

"This is both." Wade pulled a bolt cutter out of the closet and smiled. "It's a very versatile tool."

He went up to Glory's locker, snapped the lock, and handed it to Charlotte.

"For someone who rooted out corruption in the MCU," she said, tossing the lock on the table, "you play pretty loose with the law yourself."

Wade set the bolt cutters down, pulled a pair of gloves from his pocket, and put them on.

"The cops I testified against weren't bending a few legal niceties to get the job done." He opened the locker and began sorting through the contents, starting with a box of tampons and some makeup, which he set on the couch. "They were taking bribes, skimming from the cash and drugs we took as evidence, and running a protection racket out of the police department."

"This is how the corruption begins," she said.

"I'm trying to get justice for a girl who was brutally murdered and dumped like trash in a parking lot." He set a stack of gossip magazines and a cleaning uniform on the couch, then turned back to the locker for more. "I'm not trying to blackmail anybody or enrich myself."

"But once you start bending the rules," she said, "then pretty soon you starting thinking none of them matter anymore."

"That's why you're here," he said. "I wonder what she cleaned while she was wearing these."

Wade pulled out several pieces of lacy lingerie and held them up for Charlotte to examine.

She gave them a close look. "La Perla. That's not a minimum-wage brand."

"Gifts from a wealthy admirer, perhaps."

"I know what you're thinking," she said, "but just because we are in Ethan Burdett's building, that doesn't mean that he was her lover. Maybe those were for someone she was seeing after work."

"Like his son," Wade said.

"Or Timo. Or Duke Fallon or Sam Appleby. It could be anyone."

Wade gestured to the cleaning cart. "Get me a few plastic bags."

Charlotte did as she was told and came back, holding the bags open so he could drop the lingerie into them.

"I don't know why you are bothering," she said. "These are worthless as evidence by virtue of the illegal manner in which they were collected."

"I don't think virtue is going to be an issue," Wade said and slammed the locker shut.

———

"Charlotte is right," Mandy said, sitting across from Wade in a booth that Sunday morning as he worked his way through a stack of pancakes between shifts. "Just because Glory had a nightie in her locker doesn't mean that she was screwing Ethan Burdett."

"The nightie was La Perla," he said.

"Which I can get on eBay for twenty bucks. Want me to?"

"Used lingerie?" Wade asked. "Yuck."

There were only three or four others in the restaurant that morning, and they made a point of sitting as far across the restaurant as they could from Wade. He didn't take it personally.

"The locker might have been where she stashed her naughty stuff so Mom would keep on thinking that she was a good girl," Mandy said. "You should have seen what I had in my locker at school."

"You weren't a good girl?"

"I'm still not," she said. "But you already know that."

"I'm thinking that Glory brought Seth together with Timo to start moving drugs into Havenhurst," Wade said between mouthfuls of pancake. "Maybe she was even getting a cut."

"If that's true, I've got to hand it to her—she was working every angle to get out."

"Look where it got her," Wade said.

"You don't know if that's got anything to do with why she was killed. I haven't heard you mention anything that sounds remotely like a motive."

"That's mainly because I haven't come up with one yet," he said. "When did you start becoming interested in detecting?"

"When I started fucking you," she said.

"You like saying 'fucking.'"

"I like saying it because it reminds me that I'm doing it," she said.

"You can sleep with me without helping me investigate these killings."

"First off, we've shared a bed, and we've done plenty of fucking, but I haven't slept with you yet," she said. "Secondly, I have an interest in you, and you're investigating, so I want to help."

"I have an interest in you," he said, "but you don't see me making pancakes."

"I see you coming in here and eating a lot of them," she said. "Same thing."

He supposed it was.

Billy came into the restaurant and approached their booth. He was holding a folder, which he set on the table beside Wade's plate.

"This was faxed to you," he said, then nodded at Mandy. "Good morning, Ms. Guthrie."

"Billy," she said. "Please call me Mandy."

"Yes, ma'am," he said.

Wade opened the folder and started reading it.

"And never call me 'ma'am,'" she said. "It makes me feel old."

"You got it, baby," he said.

"Much better," she said.

Wade looked up at them. Billy smiled. So did Mandy, who gestured to the folder.

"What's that?" she asked.

"The autopsy report on Glory Littleton. It lays out in detail her physical condition at the time of her death and the injuries she suffered. The conclusion is that she died Monday morning of injuries consistent with a fall or blunt force trauma, specifically as a result of massive internal bleeding."

"You knew that already," Billy said.

"But there's plenty here that I didn't."

Mandy slid out of the booth. "Makes for wonderful breakfast reading."

"More like dinner," Billy said. "It's his bedtime, in case you're interested."

Both Wade and Mandy looked at him.

"What? We're all adults here," Billy said, taking Mandy's place in the booth.

"I shot you once," Wade said. "I can shoot you again."

"I keep hearing about what a dangerous place Darwin Gardens is," Billy said. "So how come you're the only who has taken a shot at me?"

"Somebody shot up your station," Mandy said.

"While it was empty, and I'm pretty sure that was Timo, acting on his own," Wade said. "Duke is giving us safe passage while we look into those dead women."

"Because it serves his interest," Mandy said.

"And because, so far, I've only been arresting junkies, sheriff's deputies, and liquor store robbers. I haven't taken a run at him yet."

"You shot up his sign," Billy said.

Wade nodded. "And since he hasn't retaliated, that tells me he's showing restraint to see how our murder investigation goes."

"What happens after that's over?" Billy asked.

Wade shrugged. "It'll be interesting to see."

Mandy put her hands on her hips and looked down at Billy. "Can I get you anything from the kitchen?"

"One of those big Injun doughnuts would be great."

Mandy turned to Wade. "You really shot him?"

"I did," Wade said.

"I don't blame you," she said, then looked back at Billy. "One *fry bread* coming right up."

"We'll take it to go," Wade said, closing the file.

"Where are we going?" Billy asked.

"Havenhurst."

Billy looked confused. "Why? When Glory was killed, Seth was on a county work detail out on the highway, under constant supervision of deputies, and his dad was in a room full of lawyers, so they're both off the hook."

"I wouldn't say that."

"Even without their kick-ass alibis," Billy said, "you haven't established a credible motive for either one of them."

"So I've been told," Wade said. "Why do you sound so lawyer-like all of a sudden?"

"I watched *Lesbian Legal 7* last night. It's the DVD I found at the station. It's like *Boston Legal*, only with lesbo action."

Wade took the file and slid out of the booth. "I've got to grab some stuff at the station. Meet me there in five minutes."

"You want to borrow the DVD?" Billy asked.

"No, thanks." Wade walked away.

"Your loss," Billy said, calling after him. "It really makes you appreciate our legal system."

CHAPTER TWENTY-THREE

Billy parked their patrol car beside Seth's Escalade in the Burdetts' motor court. The night-lights were still on and the shades were drawn. Wade figured either they were getting a late start or they weren't home. There was only one way to be sure. He got out, carrying a paper bag that looked like he'd brought along a sack lunch.

A young couple jogged past, slowing to a walk when they saw the police car. A neighbor across the street stood at the end of his driveway in his bathrobe and slippers. He'd come down to pick up the morning paper but then spotted the police and found it more interesting than reading about what the president was doing to curb the deficit.

Wade walked to the front door and rang the bell. It sounded like a symphony orchestra had been awakened into service to play the few notes.

"That's some bell," Billy said.

"It's what you get when you buy some house," Wade said.

Ethan Burdett opened the door, dressed for a game of golf.

"Oh, for God's sake," he said.

"Good morning, Mr. Burdett," Wade said. "May we come in?"

"No, you may not. Now, get the hell out of here," Ethan said. He started to close the door, but Wade stopped it with his foot.

"I'm going to be parked right in your driveway until we talk. We can do it now, inside your home, or we can do it out here, in front of your neighbors, whenever you get around to it. Makes no difference to me. But we will talk."

"I'm going to call my lawyers," Ethan said, "who are going to call the district attorney, who is going to call the chief, who will order you to get your ass off my property."

"But I won't," Wade said.

Billy smiled. He was loving this. Ethan Burdett, however, was not. Far from it.

"He'll send officers to drag you out."

"Wow," Wade said, looking back and smiling at the man in the bathrobe and the two joggers, "looks like your neighbors are in for quite a show this morning."

Gayle stepped up behind her husband and tugged at his arm.

"Ethan, please, everyone in Havenhurst is probably already wondering why the police are here. The faster we get them out of here, the better."

Ethan reluctantly stepped aside and let the officers into the dimly lit entry hall. "You are way off the reservation."

Wade was sure Ethan's choice of cliché was intentional, given that the majority of those arrested in King City were minorities, specifically Native Americans.

"My badge is good all over this city," Wade said.

"Enjoy the feeling," Ethan said, closing the door behind Billy, "because you won't be wearing it much longer."

Seth Burdett trudged down the stairs in loose sweats and a tank top that showed off his tats. He looked like he'd just rolled out of bed. His hair was askew and his eyelids were heavy.

"What do you want?" he asked.

"I got the autopsy report on Glory Littleton this morning," Wade said, "and I thought you'd all be interested in hearing the coroner's findings right away."

"Why would you think *that*?" Gayle asked. "She was our maid, not our daughter. We hardly knew her."

"Somebody knew her well," Wade said. "She was two months pregnant."

None of the Burdetts were very good at hiding their shock, although it flashed across their faces for only an instant, long enough for Wade and Billy to both spot it. The Burdetts showed an awful lot of interest for people who claimed to have none.

"I'm sorry to hear that," Ethan said. "But I fail to see what that has to do with us."

"Glory did a Lewinsky," Wade said.

"A what?" Billy asked.

"As in Monica Lewinsky," Wade said.

Billy shook his head. "Is that someone I should know?"

"Lewinsky had a sexual encounter with President Clinton and saved her semen-stained dress as a memento." Wade reached into his paper bag and pulled out a plastic evidence bag containing one of Glory's pieces of lingerie. "Glory did the same thing, saving this in her locker at Mr. Burdett's building. I guess so she'd have no trouble proving who the father of her unborn child was."

Ethan was stony faced, but Wade couldn't have gotten a more horrified expression from Gayle if he'd pulled a decapitated head out of the bag.

Seth had an entirely different reaction. He let out a sound that was as much a growl of rage as it was a cry of pain and marched right up to his father, getting nose to nose with him.

"You were fucking my woman?" Seth asked, his fists balled, but his eyes filled with tears.

Ethan took a step back, holding his hands up in front of him. "I didn't know about the two of you, but it wasn't what you think. She threw herself at me one night at the office." He looked pleadingly at his wife. "I'd had too much to drink, she was all over me, and I couldn't control myself. I'm so sorry."

Seth shoved his father hard in the chest, nearly knocking the man to the floor. Billy took a step forward, but Wade put out his hand, motioning him to stay where he was.

"Bullshit!" Seth said. "You *made* her fuck you. Because you can't let me have anything. You have to control it all."

"No, no, that wasn't how it was at all," Ethan said, scrambling back. "She was using us, don't you see? All she wanted was our seed so she could get at our money."

"Is that why you killed her?" Seth asked and launched himself at his father, pummeling him like a child instead of throwing punches, Ethan offering little resistance.

Gayle stepped back, watching the clash with a bitter smirk on her surgically wide-eyed face, her arms crossed under her stony breasts. It was almost as if she was pleased to see the fight. Wade nodded at Billy, who pulled Seth off his father without much effort.

"I didn't mean for it to happen," Ethan said, his nose bleeding, drops staining his golf shirt. "It was an accident."

"Which part? The fucking or the killing?" Seth asked, sagging weakly against Billy's hold, the fight in him gone, his anger sapped by the loss.

"Your father didn't kill Glory," Wade said, then looked at Gayle. "Your mother did."

"Wow," Billy said. "I didn't see that coming."

"Don't be absurd," Gayle said. "I had nothing to do with any of this."

"I don't know what made Glory tell you about the baby," Wade said. "Maybe you were just more irritating than usual. What did she say? Was it something like, 'Clean your own damn toilet, I'm carrying your grandchild'?"

Seth was crying softly now, and Billy let him go. Gayle turned to Ethan, who pinched his nose, stemming the trickle of blood.

"Don't just stand there," she said. "Get those men out of our house. This fiasco is over."

But Ethan stayed where he was and tilted his head back, his nose pinched, and looked at his wife without saying a word. This was Wade's show now, and Ethan was too stunned to do anything but watch it unfold.

"That must have really pissed you off," Wade continued, putting the lingerie back in the paper bag. "Were you upstairs when she mouthed off to you? Let's see."

Wade handed the bag to Billy, took a tiny flashlight from his belt, and wandered over to the staircase, aiming an ultraviolet beam at the steps, revealing a trail of previously invisible purple spots.

"Yeah, you were angry all right. It looks like you gave her a shove," he said, following the illuminated spots to a huge purple stain at the base of the stairs and purple splatter on the walls. "And gave her a few good kicks when she was down."

"That never happened," she said, shaking her head. "You're having a sick fantasy."

"The thing about blood is, just because you don't see it, that doesn't mean it's gone," Wade said. "Haven't you ever watched *CSI*? This would probably be a good time for me to remind you of your right to remain silent and that anything you say can and will be held against you. You also have right to have a lawyer present."

"I don't need a lawyer. We've lived in this house for years," Gayle said. "Those are just stains left by sloppy cleaning. If Glory did her job, they wouldn't be there. You have nothing but despicable insinuations."

"Blood doesn't lie," Wade said. "I'm sure we'll also find traces in the boat, which you used to take her body downriver to King Steel. You scraped the side of the boat on a pylon, so we'll find the paint too. You've left enough forensic evidence that the DA could have his dog try this case for him and still win."

"Jesus, Gayle," Ethan said, his voice altered by the pinched nose. "What have you done?"

"*Me*?" she asked, pointing her finger at Ethan and then at her son. "This is on the two of you. *You're* the ones who couldn't keep your pants zipped. *You're* the ones who had to get dirty with the help. I wasn't going to let that slut and your stupidity ruin this family."

Billy looked at Wade. "Maybe I'll stick with days."

"Secure the scene until the forensic unit gets here," Wade said, taking out his handcuffs. "Then come back to the station."

"Sure thing," Billy said. "Think the crime lab guys will come this time?"

"Within minutes," Wade said and stepped up behind Gayle Burdett. "Put your hands behind your back. You're under arrest."

Wade cuffed Gayle, then led her to the door past Seth, who leaned against a wall and cried, wiping the tears from his face with his arm and the Twenty-third Psalm.

——

He made a call as soon as he got Gayle stowed in the back of the squad car.

"I've arrested a suspect in Glory Littleton's murder and I'm bringing her in," he said. "You might want to spread the word."

Wade drove slowly, taking his time and using surface streets. On the way, he contacted the dispatcher, ordered a forensic unit to the Burdett house, and notified her that he'd made an arrest. He was sure those bits of news would get the chief's notice, if Ethan's lawyers hadn't contacted Reardon already.

Gayle didn't say anything when they passed through Meston Heights. All she did was frown, one of the few expressions she was still capable of despite her face-lift and Botox injections.

It wasn't until they drove through One King Plaza, passing the landmark city hall castle and heading down Division Street, that Gayle got an inkling that something was wrong.

"You've passed police headquarters," she said.

"Yes, I have."

"Where are you taking me?"

"To my station," he said.

"Darwin Gardens?" She leaned forward, nearly pressing her face against the iron mesh that separated Wade from her. "You can't. You have to take me to the station in Meston Heights. That's the one closest to where I live."

"But it's not where you dumped Glory's body," he said.

"You can't bring me there," she said. "I'm not one of those people."

He glanced up at her in the rearview mirror and met her gaze in the reflection. "I don't see a difference."

She sat back and kicked his seat again and again with both of her feet. "You can't do this!"

He ignored her.

Gayle gave up her kicking as they crossed into Darwin Gardens and looked sullenly out the window at the people milling on the sidewalks, watching the car as they passed.

The crowd grew as the car reached the intersection of Division and Arness. Just about everyone that Wade had seen outside of the King Steel factory when Glory's body was found was back on the streets again.

He made a U-turn in front of the Pancake Galaxy, where Mandy and her father stood with Ella Littleton, and pulled up in front of his station.

Gayle stared at the plywood-covered windows, which, in Wade's absence, had been freshly decorated with a spray-painted mural of a dopey-faced, smiling cop on his hands and knees, his pants pulled down, getting gleefully screwed in the ass by another cop.

"No," Gayle wailed. "I don't belong here."

Wade got out of the car, acting as if he were unaware of all the eyes on him, and walked purposefully to the sidewalk and opened the back door.

"Get out," he said.

Gayle shook her head and retreated deeper into the car. "No. I'm not going out there."

Wade reached in, grabbed her by the legs, and dragged her to the door, then yanked her up by her arms and hauled her out, kicking and twisting.

"No," she screamed. "No!"

The people on the street all got a good look at her having her tantrum. It was as clear to them as it was to her that she didn't belong there.

Wade kicked the car door shut behind him, wrapped his arms around Gayle Burdett's waist, and practically carried her into the station.

The residents of Darwin Gardens saw a lot of ugly things in their everyday lives. Junkies smoking crack and jamming syringes into their sunken flesh. People getting beaten, raped, stabbed, and murdered. Hookers giving hand jobs and blow jobs in whatever shadows they could find. Corpses decomposing on the sidewalks and in alleys and crumbling parking lots.

But they had never seen anything like this.

Which was, of course, exactly why Tom Wade did it.

CHAPTER TWENTY-FOUR

Wade was asleep in his apartment on Sunday afternoon when he was awakened by someone pounding on his door. He lay there, trying to imagine the person who went along with that knock, though it was just an excuse not to move for another moment or two. The knock sounded strong, urgent, authoritative. It was a police knock.

Billy didn't project that kind of authority, not yet, and he wouldn't leave Gayle unattended to come up to Tom's door. Charlotte had the authority, but she had no reason to be here early or to take that tone with him in her knock.

No, this was someone else.

ADA Lefcourt, perhaps? It was possible. But he didn't think she had the knuckles for the knock he was hearing.

For a moment, he thought it might be the chief, but he doubted that Reardon would come down to Darwin Gardens for Gayle Burdett, no matter how much her husband contributed to politicians in town, not with something as toxic as a murder on her head.

Wade sat up, shirtless, grabbed his cell phone, and checked the time. It was almost 1:00 p.m.

"Hold on, I'm coming," Wade said. "You don't have to break it down."

He found a pair of jogging shorts in a moving box, put them on, and went to the door, opening it to find a man standing there in a wrinkled off-the-rack suit, his hair colored an unnatural shade of brown, his thin body curled inward as if he'd taken a blow to the stomach that he'd never recovered from.

It was Detective Harry Shrake. It wasn't someone he'd expected to see, but as Wade considered Reardon's options, sending Harry down actually made a lot of sense. Harry was the perfect ambassador, someone who Wade knew well, and presumably trusted, but who was on nobody's radar outside of the department and barely registered a political blip within it.

"Afternoon, Harry," Wade said. "Come on in."

Harry stepped in and surveyed the apartment as if it were a particularly unpleasant crime scene. His gaze flitted over the yellowed walls, the moving boxes, the mattress, the newspapers on the window, the bra on the floor.

"Working nights, sleeping days, it's just like when we were rookies," Harry said. "Of course, it's easier when you're in your twenties."

Wade noticed that even Harry's eyebrows were colored. He'd never known Harry to be vain, so he figured it probably had more to do with trying to appear younger and more vital to the bureaucrats who handed out promotions.

And Harry was only thirty-eight.

"It's not so much the lack of sleep that's getting to me, Harry. The duty belts weigh a ton now. It's hell on my lower back."

"And look at how you're living." Harry went to the window, lifted the edge of newspaper that covered it, and peeked outside. "And where. Jesus, Tom, how much worse can it get? Why don't you just call it quits already?"

"Is that why you're here, Harry? To talk me into going away?"

Harry turned around and looked Wade in the eye. "I'm here because I'm taking over the Glory Littleton homicide investigation."

"The one you didn't want to touch when I called you about the body," Wade said. "Good timing, though, jumping on it now that it's solved. It won't cut too much into your workload."

"I'm bringing Gayle Burdett back downtown with me. She'll be booked there."

Wade was still sleepy, but not so much that he couldn't see the political chess moves being played on the King City board.

"So you'll be recorded as the arresting officer," Wade said.

Harry shrugged. "I'm a homicide detective, you're a beat cop. That's how it goes."

"More importantly, it goes down as a Meston Heights arrest and Darwin Gardens never has to be mentioned," Wade said. "That's assuming nobody took any pictures this morning when I brought her in, or posted them on the Internet."

Which, of course, Wade was certain that at least some people had done.

Harry shook his head. "That perp walk for the scum on Division Street was a bad call."

"It's no worse than doing it for the media outside police headquarters."

"You might think occasionally about doing what's best for the city instead of what serves your personal crusade."

"The people down here need to know that the law works for them too."

"No, they don't," Harry said. "Because they don't give a shit. They aren't the ones who pay the taxes that keep this city running. Or who fund the campaigns and cast the votes that put people in office."

"You're right," Wade said. "They're just the ones we're supposed to protect and serve."

Harry Shrake sighed and shook his head. "Now you know why you're here and you're alone and your back aches."

"Maybe so, but at least I can look at myself in the mirror," Wade said, opening the door for his former partner. "And not just because I'm wondering what shade of crap my eyebrows are."

Wade knew it was a cheap shot, but it felt good to say it anyway. He closed the door on Harry and went back to bed.

———

He slept until 8:00 p.m. and it felt like a luxury, one he'd earned by closing the Glory Littleton case. The six hours of sleep—eight if he threw in the snooze he got before Harry Shrake's visit—had reinvigorated his mind and body. He hadn't felt this alert in days.

He showered and shaved, put on his uniform, then went to his kitchen.

On his way home from New King City on Saturday, he'd stopped and bought himself some paper plates, two cereal bowls, an assortment of plastic utensils, a hundred disposable cups, and two bags of groceries.

Now he filled one of his bowls with Grape-Nuts, poured a little milk over it, and ate his dinner at the counter.

It was his first meal in his new apartment, and he liked it fine.

He used the few moments of solitude and clarity to think, going over the events of the previous day. And when he did, he saw something that he'd missed before.

Actually, he hadn't missed it. He'd seen it clearly. But it hadn't sparked the connections that it did now. And with that realization came a surprising sadness.

He wished he didn't have to do what he had to do.

But there was no hurry.

When he'd finished eating, he washed out his bowl, threw away the spoon, and went downstairs to work.

As Wade came into the station, he saw Charlotte and Billy at their desks, glowering at him. It seemed like the only thing his two officers could both agree on was their bewilderment or anger over his actions.

"You two have something you want to say?" Wade asked, facing them.

Billy spoke up first. Wade had expected Charlotte to take the lead. She seemed to enjoy chastising him.

"You let that asshole from Homicide make the collar and get all the credit for solving Glory Littleton's murder," Billy said. "That was our case."

"What matters is that her killer got caught," Wade said. "We aren't doing this for accolades."

"That's easy for you to say," Billy said. "You're at the end of your career."

"Gee, thanks," Wade said.

"The only way the two of us are getting out of here is if we can rack up some major arrests," Charlotte said, taking a more diplomatic approach.

"You haven't even been here a week and already you're planning your exit strategy?"

"We just don't want you giving the good stuff away," Charlotte said. "We'd like to get out of these uniforms someday."

"I'd like to get you out of yours today," Billy said.

"Pig," Charlotte said.

Looking at it from their position, Wade could understand their anger. They had careers to build, while he was way past caring about his. For him, it was about honoring his core principles. For them, it was about finding their way. Their objections weren't out of line.

"Fair enough," he said. "In the future, before I make a decision, I'll try to take into consideration what the unintended consequences might be for your careers."

"You might consider doing the same thing for your own," Charlotte said.

He shook his head. "Never have, never will."

"Remind me not to ask you for career advice," Billy said. "Hey, about that Lewinsky thing, was that the truth?"

"Yes, President Clinton had an affair with Monica Lewinsky," Wade said.

"No, I meant about the jizz being on Glory Littleton's panties," Billy said.

Wade shrugged. "It could be. I don't know."

"You lied," Billy said.

"I speculated," Wade said.

"I wish I could have been there for the takedown," Charlotte said. "I feel like I missed out on everything."

"That's because you work nights," Billy said. "The day shift is where the real police work is done."

———

They were on patrol, heading east on Clements Street through the center of the residential neighborhood, Wade at the wheel, putting off the inevitable.

It was a hot, humid night, the air as still and about as breathable as stone. Charlotte had the window rolled down, the movement of the car creating a breeze, but it didn't bring much relief.

She could hear a voice crackling on a loudspeaker, though they couldn't make out the words.

"What is that?" Charlotte asked.

Wade smiled, steering the car down an alley. "That'd be Mrs. Copeland."

The patrol headlights illuminated Terrill Curtis, his back to Mrs. Copeland's fence, confronting two men who were holding up an emaciated woman between them. The way the woman and two men were swaying, either they were drunk or high or there was a major earthquake going on under their feet.

In the backyard behind Terrill, Dorothy Copeland stood in a yellow floral housedress, one hand on her hip, the other holding a bullhorn in front of her mouth and aiming it like a gun at the alley.

"Go away, you filthy whore," Dorothy's voice boomed. "And take your garbage with you."

Charlotte grinned at Wade. "She loves that bullhorn."

Wade stopped the car and got out, stepping up to Terrill, who immediately backed up, holding his hands up in surrender.

"What's going on, Mr. Curtis?"

"Nothing," he said, practically whining. "I'm not doing nothing and I'm making sure they don't, either."

Terrill motioned to the threesome, who swayed to and fro, stupid grins on their faces.

"We're just having a stroll," one guy said. He had greasy hair, rheumy eyes, and a cold sore on his lip the size of the cigarette he was smoking.

"We're having a party," the woman said. She wore a tank top that hung loosely from her bony shoulders, denim shorts the size of panties, and high-heel shoes.

"Looks very festive," Wade said, then turned back to Terrill. "What's the problem?"

"You are," Terrill said. "If they take a whiz on the flowers, it's me you're gonna piss on."

"True," Wade said.

"It is?" Charlotte asked.

211

Wade ignored her and addressed the threesome. "Maybe you should take your party elsewhere."

"Sure," the woman said. "Want a blow job?"

"No, thanks," Wade said.

The three stumbled off, Charlotte watching them warily.

"They're high," she said.

"Very," Wade said.

"Shouldn't we arrest them?"

"They aren't causing any harm."

"They are publicly intoxicated," she said. "They could be a danger to themselves and to others."

"That's true," he said. "But I'll take the chance."

Dorothy approached the fence and held the bullhorn at her side.

"Thank you, officers. But that really wasn't necessary," she said, casting a smile at Terrill. "Mr. Curtis has been doing an excellent job protecting my garden. We both have."

She hefted the bullhorn to indicate how she was doing her part.

"I'm glad to hear it," Wade said.

"Do you like pecan pie?" Dorothy asked Terrill.

"I like all pie," Terrill said.

"Come inside, I've got a slice for you," she said.

Terrill was stunned. "You do?"

"But you'll have to take off your shoes and wash your hands," she said.

"Yes, ma'am," Terrill said.

Dorothy turned to the officers. "You two are welcome to join us."

"Thank you, but it will have to be another time, Mrs. Copeland. I need to pay a call on someone tonight."

Dorothy opened the padlock on the gate and let Terrill into her garden. "I'll have banana cream tomorrow."

"I'll keep that in mind," Wade said.

He and Charlotte got back into the car.

"You might as well return those lights you bought her," Charlotte said. "She's never going to give that bullhorn back to you."

"I'll get by," he said, and they drove off.

CHAPTER TWENTY-FIVE

The cots were out and Mission Possible had a full house, a captive audience for Friar Ted, who sat on a folding chair reading aloud from the Bible. No one appeared to be listening. They were talking among themselves and, in some cases, to themselves, but Ted didn't seem to mind. The preacher closed the book when he saw Wade and Charlotte approaching.

"Your audience isn't paying much attention," Wade said.

"But I'm sure they hear me," Ted said, rising to meet his guests. "God's word has a way of sinking in, even for those who think they are deaf to it. I'm living proof of that."

"I admire you for trying," Charlotte said.

"It can't do any harm," Ted said. "But I'm afraid I haven't had any luck with those photos."

"That's OK," Wade said. "That's not why I'm here. I ran into a guy today who had the Twenty-third Psalm tattooed on his arm and I thought of you."

"*Yea, though I walk through the valley of the shadow of death, I will fear no evil: for thou art with me; thy rod and thy staff, they comfort me,*" Ted recited from memory.

"*Thou preparest a table before me in the presence of mine enemies,*" Wade continued. "*Thou anointest my head with oil; my cup runneth over.*"

Ted smiled. "I'm pleased that you know it so well, and I'm sure that particular passage gives you great comfort while you're doing your job, especially here. But I don't see what made you think of me."

"Well, you've been providing meals, shelter, and comfort to street people here for two years," Wade said, "trying to show them that accepting God is the only way to be truly safe and content."

"I wish more people heard his word as clearly as you have," Ted said.

"I know you do," Wade said. "And it must be so frustrating to you when they don't."

"I can't open their hearts and minds to God. They have to do that for themselves."

"The psalm also made me think of the murders of those women that began two years ago," Wade said. "The victims were all shot with the same gun and covered with a blanket or a piece of cardboard."

"One small act of decency," Ted said.

"Or shame," Charlotte said.

"But here's the odd thing," Wade said. "They all had traces of olive oil on their heads. The kind of oil you use when giving last rites."

"Not me," Ted said. "I preach God's word, but I'm not a priest."

"But you anointed them anyway," Wade said, taking a step toward Ted, invading his personal space, "because there wouldn't have been much point in killing them without making that last effort at their salvation."

Charlotte turned and looked at Wade in astonishment.

Ted's jaw tightened, as if he'd just been given a Botox injection in his cheeks, and he held the Bible to his chest.

"You're accusing me of the worst imaginable sin," Ted said.

"Yes, I am," Wade said, and he'd been dreading it since he woke up that afternoon. "If you want to be forgiven for it, you'll confess."

"You aren't a priest either," Ted said.

Wade tried to stare him into doing the right thing, but Ted held his gaze.

Charlotte stepped up beside Wade and pointed to the men on the cots. "Everyone ignored you when you read from the Bible. Do you know why, Ted?"

"Because they are faithless and craven," he said.

"Because you can't save them, or anyone else, when you've deprived yourself of God's grace," Charlotte said. "You're carrying a horrible sin. They can sense it. That's why they don't hear you; that's why they don't believe. Anything you do here is meaningless and ineffective without his forgiveness. You know it's true."

Ted's shoulders sagged and he lowered his head in shame.

"Where's the gun, Ted?" Wade asked softly.

Ted swallowed hard. "In my room in the back, under the mattress."

Wade nodded to Charlotte, who went off to get the gun. He took out his handcuffs.

"You're under arrest, Ted," Wade said. "Put the Bible down and your hands behind your back."

Ted set the Bible down on the chair. As Wade handcuffed him and read him his rights, Ted could see that he finally had the full attention of everyone in the room.

"She was right," Ted said.

"Excuse me?" Wade said.

"May I minister to them for a few minutes?"

Wade saw everyone looking at them. "About what? The wages of sin?"

"I was thinking the blessed sanctity of forgiveness," Ted said.

"Works for me," Wade said and took a seat.

———

Wade let Ted preach for thirty minutes, his hands cuffed behind his back, to a rapt audience before taking him away.

During that time, Charlotte found the gun, as well as a vial of holy oil, in Ted's room. But before collecting those two items and putting them in evidence bags, she took detailed photographs of the room and made an inventory of everything that was in it. She also searched for anything else that might tie Ted to the crime scenes.

They brought Ted back the station and in through the back door without any of the fanfare or notice that Gayle Burdett received when she was arrested. But Wade was certain that news of the arrest would spread quickly through Darwin Gardens and that, by morning, everyone there would know about it.

Wade locked Ted in the cell, and then he and Charlotte sat down to write up their reports, which they did mostly in silence. After an hour or so, Charlotte gave Wade a copy of her paperwork and stood behind him, waiting for his reaction.

"That was quite a speech you gave to Friar Ted," he said.

"I knew all those years of Sunday school would come in handy someday."

"I'm not sure he would have broken without the push you gave him."

"He was already broken," she said. "He just had to be reminded, that's all."

They stayed at the station the rest of the night. Wade took a can of paint outside and covered over the obscene graffiti on the plywood, although he knew it was a futile effort. He decided that he'd get a window company down to replace the glass before the end of the week, even if he had to do it by force.

While he was glad to have solved the killings, he wasn't happy about the likely consequences. Mission Possible, without a passionate and devoted leader like Friar Ted, would probably close, putting a lot of homeless, hungry, and desperate people back on the streets.

And it would make it much more difficult for the next person who opened a shelter to establish credibility, much less trust, in the neighborhood.

The arrest of Friar Ted would just reinforce the rampant cynicism and distrust of institutions and authority that already existed in Darwin Gardens, especially toward anybody who came there professing a desire to do some good.

Including Wade.

At daybreak, he sent Charlotte downtown to book Ted into jail, and then he ambled over to the Pancake Galaxy when it opened to have some breakfast and a chance to flirt with Mandy.

She had a stack of hotcakes and a slice of pie waiting for him at the counter when he came in. Pete was at the register, puffing on a cigarette, his oxygen tank a few feet away.

"If I keep eating like this every day," Wade said, "I'll be the fattest cop in the department."

"Live a little," Mandy said. "You caught two murderers in twenty-four hours. That's some fancy police work, Columbo."

He took a seat at the counter. "I have my moments."

Mandy leaned close to him. "And not just in bed either."

"Thanks for getting the word out for me that I was bringing in Glory's killer."

"I didn't," Mandy said and gestured to her father. "There's your publicist."

Wade glanced at Pete, who was holding his cigarette and coughing. Each stabbing cough was deep, hard, and cutting.

"I owe you one," Wade said when Pete's coughing subsided for a moment.

"You sure like to be noticed," Pete said.

"I just want people here to know that I'm working for them."

"You're assuming they give a damn."

"You're right," Wade said.

"Then you're not half as smart as I thought you were," he said, taking another puff on his cigarette and sparking a coughing jag even worse than the one before.

Wade looked at Mandy and saw the pain on her face. It was as if she felt each cough herself.

The bell above the door jangled and Charlotte came in, carrying a manila envelope. She seemed troubled as she took the stool beside Wade.

"Did everything go OK at central booking with Ted?"

"Yes," she said.

"Did you make sure that all the paperwork reflected where the arrest was made and which team of rookie police officers closed the case?"

"Absolutely."

"So why are you looking so glum?"

She sighed. "When I was in the academy, they told us the story about those two officers who pursued a stolen car down here and drove right into an ambush."

Pete snubbed out his cigarette in an ashtray. "They took more bullets than Bonnie and Clyde."

"Our instructors ran us through a re-creation of that situation as a training exercise at the academy," she said.

"What did you learn?" Mandy asked.

"To stay the hell out of Darwin Gardens."

"I guess you flunked," Pete said.

"Things aren't going to change for you overnight," Wade said. "It's going to take a lot more than one case, and certainly not this one, to impress someone in headquarters enough to transfer you out of here."

"That's not it," she said sharply. "Give me a little credit."

"OK, sorry," he said. "So what is it?"

Charlotte slid the envelope over to him. "While I was downtown, I got the ballistics report on those guns you had me take down to the lab on my first day."

Wade opened the envelope and began to read the report, but he need not have bothered, because Charlotte already had.

"Four of the guns were used in that ambush," she said. "One of them was chrome plated. They ran the prints and came up with some names."

"Timo was one of 'em," Wade said.

"Timo Proudfoot," Charlotte said.

"No wonder he only goes by his first name."

"The others are Clay Touzee, Thomas Blackwater, and Willis Parsons."

The names meant nothing to him, of course. He needed faces.

"They're not going to let you take them without a fight," Mandy said.

"Seems likely," Wade said.

He finished his pancakes and moved on to the pie. As possible last meals go, Wade couldn't have asked for a better one.

CHAPTER TWENTY-SIX

"This is insane," Charlotte said, trying to keep up with Wade as he marched across the intersection back to the station.

"Arresting bad guys is what we do."

"But we can wait," she said. "This is big. The crime lab will surely notify the chief about what they've found. And he'll see past whatever enmity he has toward you and send a tactical force down here to seek justice for those two dead officers."

"That's what I'm afraid of."

"Because you want to bring down Timo yourself."

Wade stopped on the sidewalk and faced her. "Because it will be the equivalent of a military invasion. A lot of people who had nothing to do with that massacre will die on both sides."

"It won't be our fault," she said.

"But it will ignite so much hatred that no one in King City will ever put a human face on Darwin Gardens again and it will make it impossible for a cop here to ever earn anyone's trust."

"And that matters to you?"

"This is my home," he said.

"It wasn't a week ago," she said.

"It is now." Wade turned and burst into the station so suddenly, and in such a hard-charging manner, that he startled Billy, who was in the midst of opening a package of Oreos. Billy ripped the package wide open and the cookies went flying.

"What the hell?" Billy asked.

"Grab a shotgun and extra ammo," Wade said to him, then pointed to Charlotte. "Get us pictures of the guys who match the fingerprints on those guns."

"What are we doing?" Billy asked as he went to the gun locker and Charlotte went to the computer on her desk.

"We're arresting Timo Proudfoot and the other assholes who gunned down those two rookies here a few years ago," Wade said.

"Hot damn," Billy said and tossed Wade a shotgun, which he caught with one hand. "I love the day shift."

"Where do we find them?" Charlotte asked. The pages with photos of Timo Proudfoot, Clay Touzee, Thomas Blackwater, and Willis Parsons spit out of the printer behind her.

"We'll start at Headlights, Duke's strip club," Wade said. He took several clips for his gun and a handful of shells and stuck them in his pockets. Billy did the same. "We'll go in three cars. They won't be expecting us, so that's one advantage."

Charlotte joined them at the gun locker, handed out the photographs, then took a shotgun for herself and some extra ammo.

Billy glanced at the pictures. "Four desperados, wanted dead or alive."

He hadn't seen them before, but Charlotte had, outside of Headlights the last time she was there. Wade glanced at the photos too, and recognized them all from his encounter on the street.

"What's the plan?" Charlotte asked.

"I'll take the front," he said. "You two take the back."

She nodded, pocketing her extra clips. "Are you sure you aren't overthinking this?"

But her words bounced off Wade's back. He was already heading out the door to the patrol cars.

———

Wade sped down Weaver Street, Billy and Charlotte following right behind him like they were in a parade.

He took out his cell phone, asked directory assistance for the number for Headlights, and then had the operator connect him at no additional charge.

A man answered. "Yeah?"

"How's business this morning?"

"It's nine thirty. How many people you know go to a tittie bar for breakfast?"

"So I'd have no trouble getting a table," Wade said.

"What the fuck you want?"

"I'd like to speak to Timo, please," Wade said. "Tell him it's Tom Wade."

The man set the phone down and called out for Timo. Weaver Street ended in a T intersection with Curtis Avenue. Headlights was on Curtis, facing Weaver. Wade could see it right in front of him.

"What do you want?" Timo asked.

"You there with your buddies, plotting mischief?"

"We're taking turns with Brooke," Timo said. "She's on the floor. Her legs are spread and she's begging us for more in every hole she's got. Like she does for her daddy."

Wade stepped on the gas. "I know you killed those two cops a few years back."

"Then you know what I'm gonna do to you as soon as I'm done with her."

"Are you going to surrender?" He steered the car so the front door of Headlights was in the center of his grill and closed in fast.

"Fuck you," Timo said.

"I was hoping you'd say that."

Wade drove through the door like a wrecking ball, taking down most of the front wall in an explosion of wood, plaster, and glass. His car plowed through tables and chairs and into the stage, snapping the strippers' poles.

The bar was to his right. Wade got out of the car, his gun at his side.

Timo popped up from behind the bar with a shotgun, let out a furious wail, and simultaneously fired both barrels at Wade, but the car took the hit.

Wade returned fire. Timo ducked down, and the mirror behind the bar shattered.

A door to Wade's left flew open and Thomas Blackwater came out firing. Wade shot him in the chest, blowing him back into the room, then continued his advance on the bar, working his way through the rubble.

He heard some more shots outside, but he kept on going. Charlotte and Billy would have to take care of themselves. A dangling glass shard hanging from the mirror frame on the wall showed Wade a skewed reflection of the area behind the bar.

He saw the bottles, the sinks, the rags, and the rubber mats on the floor, covered with broken glass.

Timo wasn't there.

He leaned over the counter and saw something he didn't see in the reflection. There was a trapdoor on the floor. It was open, a ladder leading to a storeroom below.

Something stirred behind him. He whirled around, gun drawn, to find Charlotte standing in the doorway to the back room. She was breathing hard, her face dappled with beads of sweat. He could hear someone screaming in agony outside.

"What's the situation?" Wade asked.

"All clear. Blackwater is dead and Touzee is wounded, shot in the gut. Billy's got Parsons and one other facedown on the ground and is reading them their rights. You?"

"Timo got away," he said. Outside, they could both hear a car burning rubber. "That'd be him."

"What do we do now?" Charlotte asked.

"Call dispatch, tell them what we have," Wade said as he retraced his steps back through the rubble to his car. "Wait here for the medical examiner, the ambulance, and the detectives to arrive."

He got into his car.

"Wait a minute," she said. "Where are you going?"

"Same place as Timo," he said. "The Alphabet Towers."

"That's insane. It's a fortress. You don't stand a chance against them all."

"I don't want them all," he said. "I just want Timo."

He backed the car up the way he came in and charged southbound on Curtis Avenue, dragging his front bumper against the asphalt and leaving a trail of sparks.

It wasn't until he was closing in on Timo's Escalade, and could see the three Alphabet Towers looming in the distance, that he felt the blood trickling down his leg and the deep sting in his thigh. Either a bullet had grazed his leg or he'd taken a little buckshot. Either way, it wouldn't slow him down much.

They were nearly at the towers when Wade tried to edge past Timo on the Escalade's driver's side. Timo swerved toward him and the two cars slammed together in a shower of sparks and screeching metal.

Timo sped ahead and Wade let him, until the patrol car's left front edge was beside the Escalade's right rear bumper.

That's when Wade executed a routine pursuit intervention technique maneuver, clipping the edge of the SUV.

On most cars, this simple action, when properly done, will spin the fleeing vehicle sideways in front of the patrol car, allowing it to be rammed.

But since SUVs are heavy and have a higher center of gravity than most vehicles, the PIT maneuver can have another, more devastating effect.

Which it did this time.

The Escalade fishtailed, flipped, and rolled down the street, jumping the curb in front of the Alphabet Towers and flattening the wrought iron fence.

The armed sentries scattered to avoid being crushed by the tumbling Escalade before it finally came to rest on its side, crumbled and smoking, ten yards shy of the entrance to Tower B.

Wade parked his car at the curb, drew his gun, and strode up to the vehicle. The Escalade was smashed up and bleeding gasoline, but otherwise, it was intact.

And unoccupied.

The windshield was kicked out and a few drops of blood led from the Escalade to the front door of Tower B.

Wade looked up at Duke Fallon's penthouse on the twentieth floor and he thought about all the stairs, all the people, and all the guns that stood between him and knocking on Duke's front door.

So he walked back to his car, popped the trunk, and took out a road flare.

He pulled the cap off the flare, struck the scratch tip, and ignited it, sparking a hissing flame that was like a blowtorch.

The sentries were beginning to regroup and move back toward him when Wade tossed the flare into the trail of gasoline that was leaking from the Escalade and ducked behind his squad car.

"Motherfucker!" one of the sentries yelled, and they all scattered again.

The flames roared along the fuel trail like a lit fuse and into the undercarriage of the Escalade. The SUV exploded in a red-hot fireball of glass and metal that rose from the ground and into air like a fist of flame and then landed again.

Wade stood, gun at his side, and walked past the flaming wreckage to the entrance of the tower.

And waited.

He didn't move as the sentries, and some of the residents, closed in behind him, blocking the path between him and his car. They carried guns, knives, chains, lead pipes, and untapped reservoirs of hatred and resentment. There would be no turning back, but he knew that even before he'd left the station.

Within a few moments, an enraged Duke Fallon burst out of the building in one of his expensive tracksuits and holding a gun in each hand. He was flanked by half a dozen very muscular, very angry, and very armed men.

Wade held his ground.

"This shit will not be tolerated," Duke yelled, gesturing with one of his guns at the burning car. "This is my fucking house you're disrespecting and that disrespects me."

Wade shrugged it off. "You think this is bad? It's nothing compared to the tidal wave that's about to sweep through here and wipe you out of existence."

Duke laughed and pressed his gun to Wade's forehead. "Is that what you think you are?"

"It's not me you have to worry about."

"That's for damn sure," Duke said, "especially after I put a bullet in your head."

"The chief knows that Timo was one of the assholes who killed those rookie cops that were slaughtered here. Before the day is out, the chief is going to come and get him with all the men and firepower the department has got. And if you make the chief do that, he won't stop with just one man, not with a dozen TV news choppers overheard. He'll have to put on a good show for them. So he'll scorch the earth of you and every insect that's crawling on this toxic patch of dirt that you consider your kingdom. The horsemen of the apocalypse are coming, and the only hope you have of stopping them is by giving me Timo."

Duke glowered at Wade for a long moment before lowering his gun and turning to one of his guards.

"Give me a fucking phone," Duke said. The guard held a cell phone out to him. Duke traded it for one of his guns and made a call. "Send Timo down here now."

Duke pocketed the phone.

An instant later, Wade heard a scream of such unmitigated terror that it made him shiver. He looked up and saw Timo plummeting from one of the upper floors, his arms and legs flailing.

As Timo's body dropped through the air, his scream became louder and almost musical, conveying with bone-chilling intensity the betrayal, disbelief, and mindless terror that he felt as he stared down at his unstoppable fate.

Timo's body smacked into the burning Escalade and burst like a water balloon filled with guts. There was a loud hiss as the moisture hit the jagged, red-hot metal and the air filled with the coppery, acrid stench of burning flesh.

There were more screams and wails, from within the crowd and from the scores of onlookers drawn to the windows and balconies of the tower above, but none were as haunting as Timo's final cry.

Wade almost felt sorry for him.

"Are we done here?" Duke asked. "I don't want to miss *Dancing with the Stars*."

Wade nodded and Duke went back inside.

CHAPTER TWENTY-SEVEN

The King City Police rolled into Darwin Gardens, but not in the numbers or with the force that would have accompanied a search for cop killers and aroused the widespread interest of the news media.

Outside the Alphabet Towers, a special weapons and tactical team formed a defensive perimeter around Timo's Escalade, and a police chopper circled overhead, to ensure the safety of the authorities processing the crime scene. Another SWAT team did the same thing at Headlights, though they need not have bothered. The residents of Darwin Gardens, and those in Duke Fallon's direct employ, remained inside and out of sight, doing nothing that might provoke the police.

There was no media presence because the public didn't care about crime in Darwin Gardens and the department didn't make it seem like anything more than business as usual. It wasn't newsworthy or surprising that the police sent SWAT teams to protect the officers who were cleaning up after yet another murder in that hellhole. It was common sense.

Chief Reardon certainly wasn't going to reveal that the shooters of the two rookie cops years ago had actually slipped through the massive, and bloody, police offensive in Darwin Gardens that immediately followed the ambush.

Or that it was Tom Wade, the man who'd exposed widespread corruption of the MCU, who'd finally solved the case. Or that Wade had done so mere hours after capturing a serial killer that the department didn't even know existed.

But with Clay Touzee and Willis Parsons, two of the cop killers, in custody and Friar Ted confessing to multiple murders, Chief Reardon wouldn't be able to keep things quiet for long.

Wade was certain that the chief spent his afternoon huddled with the district attorney, trying figure out how to spin the facts so that, when they quietly came out, they showed the department in the best possible light and downplayed, if not completely eliminated, the roles played by Wade and his two officers.

Not that Wade cared. He didn't want the attention or need the vindication.

It was satisfaction enough for him that the chief, the police department, and the people of Darwin Gardens knew the truth of what had happened.

It wasn't until that night, after all the forensic evidence had been gathered, after all the bodies had been taken away, and after all the reports had been filed, that Tom Wade, Charlotte Greene, and Billy Hagen finally got together again at the station without anyone else around.

They sat at their desks, facing one another, exhausted by it all. But Wade knew it had been especially stressful for Charlotte and Billy. They'd just been through their first gunfight, and one of them had gut shot a suspect, enduring his screams of agony until the paramedics took him away.

Wade didn't know which one of his officers had fired the shot, and he couldn't tell from the expressions on their faces. They both looked emotionally and physically wiped out.

Billy gestured to the bloodstained tear on Wade's right pant leg. "Did you get hit?"

"Just a scratch," he said, though it was one that had required a few stitches to close up, but he saw no reason to tell them that. "Are you both OK with how things went down today?"

"Hell no," Charlotte said.

Wade glanced at Billy. "How about you?"

"I'm cool with it," Billy said. "We took care of business."

Wade nodded and looked back at Charlotte. "So what was your problem?"

"You," she said.

"What did I do?"

"You drove through the fucking door."

"It gave us the element of surprise," he said.

"It certainly surprised me," Billy said.

"That's the problem, Billy," she said. "*They* should have been surprised, not us. We should have known exactly what our leader was going to do and been prepared for it. But he couldn't tell us his plan because he was making it up as he went along."

"I told you I'd take the front," Wade said. "And I did."

"But you didn't tell us you were going to drive your car into the middle of the club and come out shooting," Charlotte said.

"You can do all the planning you want, but it doesn't mean shit once you are out there. You aren't in control of everything. Situations change and you have to be flexible. You can't rely on the plan to carry you through. So I plan very loosely."

"You don't plan at all," she said. "And that put you and the two of us at greater risk than we needed to be."

Wade looked over at Billy. "Do you feel the same way that she does?"

Billy shook his head. "I was fine with everything but the screaming."

So now Wade knew who'd shot Clay Touzee.

"It's always difficult to see someone suffering," Wade said. "But know this—you shot him because he was shooting at you. You didn't cause his pain. He brought it on himself."

"I'm glad he was hurting," Billy said.

"You were?"

"The bastard had it coming," Billy said.

"So it was just the noise that got on your nerves?"

"I shot to kill and I missed," Billy said. "All that screaming meant that the son of a bitch still had plenty of gas in him to keep shooting at me, or you, or Charlotte."

"But he didn't," Charlotte said.

"Only because he dropped his gun when he got hit and it landed out of reach," Billy said. "If he hadn't, things might have turned out differently. I let you both down."

"No, you didn't," Wade said. "Neither of you did. I know you both have my back and I'm proud to have you as my partners."

"If that's true," Charlotte said, "then you shouldn't have gone to the towers alone."

"It was the only way," Wade said.

"You mean it was the only way for *you*," she said.

"You just had to blow up Timo's ride," Billy said.

Wade shrugged. "It seemed like the right thing to do at the time."

"What do you have against cars?" Billy asked.

"Nothing," Wade replied.

"C'mon, Sarge, you've been trashing them, shooting them, and blowing them up since you got here," Billy said. "Did a car run over your dog or something when you were a kid?"

"I've only blown up one car," Wade said.

"And you smashed your own with a tire iron," Charlotte said.

"He did?" Billy said.

"Right out there on the street. Pete told me," Charlotte said. "There's definitely some psychological issue at work here."

"It will give you something to think about at home," Wade said and stood up. "Get out of here, both of you. We're done."

"Technically, my shift hasn't started yet," Charlotte said.

"And mine isn't over," Billy said.

"We're taking the night off," Wade said.

"What if something comes up?" Charlotte said.

"Nothing will," he said.

"Duke Fallon could come gunning for you," Billy said.

"He might," Wade said. "But not tonight."

He looked past them to see Mandy coming in the front door, holding a stack of three pie cartons.

"Dad and I thought you guys could use something sweet after what you've been through today," Mandy said. "There's a pie here for each of you."

Wade wondered what the fascination was with pies in Darwin Gardens. They seemed to be a big part of the local culture. Between Duke, Mandy, Pete, and Mrs. Copeland, pie did heavy duty as a panacea, a metaphor, a token of affection, and even a currency of sorts.

"Thank you," Charlotte said and took a carton off the top. "That's very kind."

She headed off and Billy stepped up, taking the next carton off Mandy's hands.

"I've heard that your apple pie is an aphrodisiac," he said.

"I wouldn't know," Mandy said. "I've never needed the assistance."

"I'll take every edge I can get," Billy said, nodded his thanks to Mandy, and left.

That left Wade and Mandy alone with their pie. She held the carton out to him.

"What about you, big guy?" she asked. "Do you need some help in that department?"

Wade stepped past her, closed the door, and locked it. Then he came up behind her, cupped her breasts in his hands, and whispered his intentions in her ear, all the things he'd wanted to do to her the other morning. She dropped the carton on a desk and leaned against him, her head resting on his shoulder.

"No," she said, her voice husky in his ear. "You don't need it."

———

Tom Wade's second week in Darwin Gardens was far less eventful than the first. He and his two officers made a few arrests for tagging, possession, and sale of narcotics, and for lewd, drunk, and disorderly conduct, but there were no robberies, drive-by shootings, rapes, murders, or other major felonies to deal with.

Wade figured it was because the people in Darwin Gardens were in a kind of shock, uncertain how to interpret everything that had happened, all that had changed, and what it meant for the future.

Although he knew that Timo was thrown off the building on Duke's orders, Wade couldn't prove that it wasn't an accident or suicide.

But everyone knew the truth.

The widely held belief in Darwin Gardens—according to Mandy, anyway—was that the startling brutality of Timo's execution was intended to terrorize the community, to remind everyone of Duke's power and his wrath.

Duke also couldn't risk a police invasion or for detectives to get their hands on someone who knew so much about his operation.

More important, Duke had to do something big to firmly assert his position and relevance in the new neighborhood order, one that now included Tom Wade, who had managed in a few short days to establish his own authority and even win a measure of respect.

The people knew what Wade had done for them. They knew it because they'd seen it. His actions told them the kind of man that he was, not just by how he enforced the law, but in the way that he lived.

It also didn't hurt that he'd stood up to Duke Fallon and walked away alive.

The big, unanswered question now was if it was possible for Duke Fallon and Tom Wade to coexist in Darwin Gardens without forcing people to declare allegiance to one of them and sparking a street war.

Wade didn't have the answer.

He could only do his job and hope that everything worked out.

So he took advantage of the relative quiet, putting Charlotte and Billy to work with him repairing and remodeling the station. The rookies groused about doing "home improvement" instead of policing, but Wade thought it was important labor. He wanted them to feel that the station belonged to them and he hoped that sense of belonging would extend to the street outside as well. While the interior of the station was improving, he still hadn't been able to get a window company down to replace the glass, and he was losing his patience.

Between shifts, Wade got a lot of sleep, some of it beside Mandy, and always in his bed, not hers. He didn't even know where she lived and hadn't bothered to ask, not that Mandy seemed the slightest bit offended by his apparent lack of interest in her life. If anything, his simple acceptance of her as she was and for whatever she was willing to give only made him more attractive to her.

It was a good week, and it went by quickly. Before he knew it, Saturday had come along. He turned in his rented Explorer, picked up his Mustang, now minus all of the *Bullitt* crap, and headed out to New King City to spend the day with his daughter.

CHAPTER TWENTY-EIGHT

This time, he didn't feel like he was leaving a bad dream, but rather, that he was living a double life, one in Darwin Gardens and another in New King City, and that King's Crossing had become the physical and temporal bridge between the two.

It felt good to be back in his own car, so much so that he listened to his Neil Diamond CD without feeling any of the usual embarrassment. He liked Neil and he was going to own it. Fuck anybody who had a problem with that. He pulled into his driveway with the windows down and "Solitary Man" blaring from the speakers.

Wade got out of the car and strode up to the front door. Brooke opened it and came out dragging a rolling suitcase and holding a sleeping bag under one arm.

"Whoa," Wade said. "What's all this?"

"I'm spending the weekend with you," she said. "I'm sure you need some help unpacking."

"Slow down," Wade said. "I told you I'd think about it. I haven't decided yet."

"I have," she said.

"This is a discussion we need to have with Mom."

"Not me, you," she said and went right past him to the car. "I'll be in the car."

He watched her go, once again finding himself torn between pride and irritation. But he could see already that her teenage years, especially once she started dating and got her driver's license, were going to be a living hell for him.

Wade turned and went into the house. Nothing had really changed since he'd left. Even when he'd lived there, he'd never been allowed to have a say in decorating any room except the garage. The only familiar piece missing in the house was him.

He found Alison in the kitchen, sitting at the table, nursing a cup of coffee.

"You didn't tell me you were living in Darwin Gardens," she said.

"And you're mad at me that you had to hear it from Brooke first," he said, sitting down across from her. "I really am sorry about that, and I don't blame you for being angry. I'm going to work a lot harder at communicating with you about things. That's a promise."

She nodded. "Did you invite her to spend the weekend with you?"

"No, of course I didn't," he said. "This is entirely her doing. She's trying to press the issue because she's curious about where I live. I told her that it isn't safe for her there, and you know what she said? If she's not safe in Darwin Gardens with an armed police officer at her side, then she's not going to be safe anywhere."

"She's right," Alison said.

"She is?"

"Brooke loves you, and if that's where you live, then she wants to be there too."

"It's Darwin Gardens, Ally."

"I don't care where it is," Alison said. "It's your home, and it's not going to be much of one if your daughter isn't a part of it. Put her to work painting or something. She'll love it."

Investing his daughter in his home the way he'd invested his officers in the station. Alison was thinking about things the same way he was. It shouldn't have been such a surprise to him. There was a lot of common ground between them, or they wouldn't have fallen in love or been married for so many years.

"Aren't you worried about her safety?" he asked.

"Of course I am. Constantly. But if she's with you, I know that she's safe."

Wade didn't know what to say. He'd been prepared for a confrontation and to uncharacteristically surrender without a fight. But he hadn't prepared for this.

Alison smiled. "You were expecting me to be a hard-ass about this, weren't you?"

"It would have helped."

"I know you, Tom, and why you're living down there. I'm not so sure that Brooke does. I want her to be in your life, to know you and what you believe. I will never stand in the way of that. Taking her out for burgers and movies once a week isn't going to cut it."

"Thanks, Ally, but I really wasn't ready for this. It's going to be damn awkward."

"Life usually is," she said. "It'll be good for both of you."

Wade wasn't sure what he was going to do with Brooke during his shifts or how to deal with her and his relationship with Mandy.

He suddenly had a troubling thought.

Did Mandy leave her bra on the floor again? Were there plastic cups lying around with lipstick on the rim? Did his bed look like two people had slept in it? Did his place reek of sex?

He'd definitely have to stall Brooke in the station while he went upstairs and cleaned up any incriminating evidence in his apartment.

He got up. "Yeah, I'm sure it will be."

"I'll try not to call every hour to check on her," she said.

"I appreciate your confidence," he said.

"Maybe every other hour."

"Works for me," he said.

———

Brooke, for all of her bravado, slunk down in her seat as they rolled into Darwin Gardens. She'd never been anywhere as bleak, decayed, and forgotten as this. The signs of crime and neglect were everywhere.

"Having second thoughts?" Wade asked.

"I'd be crazy not to," she said. "But no, I want to see this. I can't hide from this stuff forever."

That was true, and he began to question the wisdom of keeping her shielded from so much for so long.

"But do you want to live with it?" he asked.

"You do," she said.

"I'm paid to."

"Not to live here, you're not. You made that choice."

And he could tell that she was wondering how he could have made that insane decision. When he woke up each day to his piss-yellow walls and stained carpets, he sometimes wondered the same thing.

As they neared the station, he saw a truck carrying plates of glass parked outside and two workers inside, just behind the wrought iron bars, installing windows where the plywood had been.

He didn't believe for one second that anyone at One King Plaza was willing to spend money on an outpost they didn't care about, much less go to the trouble of arranging for workers to come on a weekend.

For a moment, he thought it might be the chief's small way of acknowledging the good work that Wade and his team had done in their first week, but Wade quickly dismissed the notion. The chief didn't want to encourage them to do any further police work. He wanted them to go away.

So where did the window installers come from? Could it have been Claggett, his landlord, who'd arranged it? If so, Wade would have him send the bill to One King Plaza and hope for the best.

Wade pulled the Mustang into the back lot and parked beside Billy's Chevy convertible. He took his daughter's sleeping bag and led her inside.

Billy was at his desk and sat up quickly, startled to see a child in the station, wheeling a suitcase.

"Brooke," Wade said, "this is Officer Hagen. He works with me here."

"Call me Billy," he said, offering Brooke his hand. She gave it a surprisingly firm shake and glanced at her father for approval.

"You can call him whatever he likes," Wade said, tossing the sleeping bag on his desk. "But remember that he's a police officer and do what he tells you, especially if I am not around."

"Pleased to meet you, Billy," she said. "Are you sure you're old enough to be a cop? You don't look much older than me."

"Youthful good looks is a family curse," he said, then caught Wade watching the workers. "How did you get those guys to come down here?"

"I didn't," Wade said and then approached one of the two workers, a heavy Native American who wore thick work gloves and a white jumpsuit and was fitting a sheet of glass into place with suction cups. "Excuse me."

The worker stopped what he was doing and regarded Wade. "Yes, sir?"

"It's great that you're here. Do you mind if I ask who's paying for all of this?"

The worker tipped his head toward the Pancake Galaxy across the street. "Mr. Fallon."

That's when Wade noticed Fallon's Mercedes parked on the Arness Street side of the restaurant. He thought about the situation for a moment, then came to a decision.

"Thanks," he said, then looked over at Brooke. "Stay here with Billy for a minute. He'll show you around. I need to have a talk with someone."

"Sure," she said.

Wade strode across the street and went into the restaurant. There were about a dozen patrons, but none of them acknowledged him when he came in, perhaps because Duke Fallon was there, sitting in a booth in the back, eating a slice of pie.

Of course he was.

Mandy and Pete were at the counter. He smiled at them as he passed on his way to Fallon's booth.

"Good morning, Duke. May I join you?"

Duke had a napkin tucked into the collar of his tracksuit and another one on his lap. He wasn't taking any chances on staining himself this time.

"I wish you would," Duke said. "It'd make my life a lot easier."

"That's not why I'm here," Wade said.

"I've noticed," Duke said, then gestured for him to sit down.

Wade slid into the booth across from him. Mandy came over with a pot of coffee and an empty mug. She set the mug down in front of Wade and filled it up without waiting to be asked.

"Thank you, Mandy," Wade said and took a sip.

"She's getting to know all your preferences," Duke said.

"That's how a good waitress earns big tips," she said and winked at Wade. It made him uncomfortable, and that made her and Duke smile.

"Can I buy you a slice of pie?" Duke asked him.

"No, thanks, I'm trying to cut down," Wade said and watched Mandy as she went back to the counter and joined her father.

"This is the first time I've seen you out of uniform," Duke said.

"But I see you're still wearing yours," Wade said. "Why'd you send those guys over to replace our windows?"

"It was an eyesore," Duke said.

"You got a problem with plywood illustrated with cops giving it to each other up the ass?"

"We can't have our police station looking like a condemned building."

Our police station. It struck Wade as an interesting choice of words. He had some more of his coffee while he pondered it.

"I don't know if I can accept your generosity."

"Sure you can."

"Accepting gifts from felons is what got the MCU in trouble," Wade said. "Believe me, I ought to know."

"It's not a payoff or a bribe. It's reparations. I may have been indirectly responsible for the damage that was done, so it's only right that I should fix it."

"I'm glad to hear you're interested in doing the right thing."

"Besides, the station doesn't belong to you. It belongs to the community."

Wade couldn't argue with that, and he appreciated the sentiment, even if it was coming from a murderer, a drug dealer, an extortionist, and a pimp.

"Well, Duke, when you put it that way, all I can do is thank you."

"It's my pleasure," Duke said.

And Wade knew that if word got around that Duke installed the glass, and it surely would, then nobody would risk tossing a brick through it or shooting it up. Duke was bringing Wade under his protection, only without the weekly fee he imposed on all of the other merchants in Darwin Gardens.

"You're almost making me feel welcome," Wade said.

"You are," Duke said. "Within limits."

"We'll see about that."

"I'm sure we will," Duke said, then pointed across the street with his fork. "Who's that little girl?"

Wade followed his gaze and saw Brooke and Billy in the station through the gleaming, newly installed window.

"My daughter," Wade said. "I have her for the weekend."

Duke looked at Wade as if seeing him for the first time. "You brought her *here*?"

"This is where I live," Wade said.

Duke finished up his pie and started working on the crumbs. Mandy came over with the coffeepot and freshened their cups.

"You know something, Tom?" Duke said. "I like you a hell of a lot better when you aren't wearing a badge."

"I'm always wearing it, Duke."

"I think he was born with one," Mandy said.

"You poor bastard," Duke said and shook his head at Wade. "It's going to be the death of you some day."

Wade nodded and took a sip of his coffee. "I wouldn't want it any other way."

About the Author

 Lee Goldberg is a two-time Edgar Award nominee who has written and produced scores of highly successful network television series, including *Diagnosis Murder, Spenser: For Hire, Baywatch, SeaQuest, Hunter, Nero Wolfe, Martial Law, Missing, Monk,* and *The Glades.*

He's also the author of over thirty novels and non-fiction books, including *The Walk, Watch Me Die, Successful Television Writing, My Gun Has Bullets,* the long-running *Diagnosis Murder* and *Monk* series of original mystery novels, and the new Dead Man series of monthly horror-thrillers for Amazon's 47North Imprint.

As an international television consultant, he has advised networks and studios in Canada, France, Germany, Spain, China, Sweden, and the Netherlands on the creation, writing, and production of episodic television series.

Goldberg lives in Los Angeles with his wife and daughter and is already hard at work on the further adventures of Tom Wade.

GOLDB
Goldberg, Lee,
King City /

HEIGHTS
08/12